"YOU'RE A WILD ROSE AND YOUR THORNS CUT DEEP AT TIMES, NICOLE . . . BUT NO FLOWER IS MORE DESIRABLE."

He clinked his glass to hers and took a long sip of the amber liquid. Without warning, his lips were upon hers in a kiss so tender that it could not but melt the cold place that she jealously guarded deep within her.

As of its own volition her mouth answered his, probing, bruising, needing. Then, as suddenly as he began kissing her, he ended. The taste of champagne lingered upon her lips.

WILD ROSES

Sheila Paulos

A CANDLELIGHT ECSTASY ROMANCE™

Published by
Dell Publishing Co., Inc.
1 Dag Hammarskjold Plaza
New York, New York 10017

Dell ® TM 681510, Dell Publishing Co., Inc.

Candlelight Ecstasy Romance™ is a trademark of
Dell Publishing Co., Inc., New York, New York.

ISBN: 0-440-19728-7

Printed in the United States of America
First printing—January 1983

To Our Readers:

We have been delighted with your enthusiastic response to Candlelight Ecstasy Romances™, and we thank you for the interest you have shown in this exciting series.

In the upcoming months we will continue to present the distinctive sensuous love stories you have come to expect only from Ecstasy. We look forward to bringing you many more books from your favorite authors and also the very finest work from new authors of contemporary romantic fiction.

As always, we are striving to present the unique, absorbing love stories that you enjoy most—books that are more than ordinary romance.

Your suggestions and comments are always welcome. Please write to us at the address below.

Sincerely,

The Editors
Candlelight Romances
1 Dag Hammarskjold Plaza
New York, New York 10017

WILD ROSES

CHAPTER ONE

Nickie Alexander sucked in her breath as her eyes passed quickly over the score of half-naked men who surrounded her. Each one had a physique to put Adonis to shame, and each one a leer on his face that made her wince.

Plucking up her courage, she turned to Gordon Martins, the hitter who almost lost the game for the Seattle Vikings, a young expansion club that was one of the fastest rising baseball teams in recent history. She held out her microphone toward him.

"Why, Gordon, did you turn a sure double into a chancy triple, to make the second out of the ninth inning? There's an old saying in baseball that it's good to be fast, but it's better to be smart."

Gordon Martins looked at her in astonishment, too taken aback to answer in anything other than an incoherent mumble. The leer on the face of the second player interviewed, a second-string pitcher, quickly disappeared as Nickie, who would broadcast this later to the fifty thousand listeners of her radio station, took him to task for showing off with a trick pitch, thus allowing the opposing team to score their only run of the game. The amused jocularity of the team at having a female, a young, pretty one at that, break down the male bastions of the clubhouse for an on-the-spot interview gave way, she sensed, to a grudging respect and discomfort.

Upon first entering the pungently scented clubhouse, the first woman ever to do so, the swarm of bare chests and buttocks wrapped tightly in Turkish towels had made her instantly regret her decision. It was easy to be bold and casual before the fact, but despite her studied offhandedness and sophistication, Nickie was tense. Although teams legally had to open their locker rooms to women, thanks to a lawsuit filed a few years ago by a woman reporter against the Yankees, no judge was forcing them to be nice. Having remembered the item about one female reporter who was greeted by a barrage of soggy french fries from an angry team, Nickie had been more than a little apprehensive about coming here. She had been terrified. It was exactly one month today that she had gotten this job as sportscaster on WRPJ, a local Seattle station that was known for its sports coverage. Nickie was aware that despite her superior ability and knowledge, the only reason she had been hired was that she was a woman, and the station had wanted to appease local equal rights groups. The station manager and the crew were waiting for her to fail, so they could hire the man they had wanted in the first place. Well, they would have a long time to wait. Nickie set her jaw determinedly at the thought. She was going to make it, and make it big. She had to. She had nothing else.

Up until today she had gotten her news routinely from press releases, from the wire services, or as a spectator. Her break had come through her uncle Ned, whose old school chum had just bought Seattle's new baseball team. He had been only too glad to do a favor for his friend by allowing his niece entry to the clubhouse, thereby giving her career a badly needed boost. She hadn't known how the players would react to anyone in there with them right after a big game, let alone a woman. It was turning out to be not as bad as she had feared, if she ignored the smirks. At least the men were answering her questions. As Nickie interviewed her third and then her fourth player, her palms began to dry a bit, and the realization that these were only men, albeit well-built, coordinated ones, dawned on her with a thud.

"Cooper, did you have permission to steal second, or did you do it on your own?" she shot out.

"And Costello, how would rate your timing this season?" Nickie was in form.

Tall, lithe, with long jet-black curls and huge cobalt-blue eyes, looking more as if she belonged in the viewfinder of a photographer's lens than in the Vikings' clubhouse, she was nonetheless in control. She knew it and they knew it. Costello stuttered as he answered. Some of the other players who, amused, had formed a tight circle around Nickie as she began her interview began now to casually drift away. That was all right. Her interview was, thus far, brisk and to the point. She didn't want to drag it out and risk boring her listeners. All she needed to top off her segment was a brief session with Craig Boone, the Vikings' ace starting pitcher. Getting that interview would not be easy. Boone was notoriously, and some said unsportingly, hostile to the media. Celebrity was anathema to him. He claimed that if he wanted to be in show business he would have been a song-and-dance man. All he wanted to do was to play ball. Somehow Nickie was not bothered by that. Her success had thus far infused her with a sense that she could not fail. She was not, he would see, your run-of-the-mill hack reporter. Like Boone himself, grit, talent, and a measure of luck had gotten her to where she was.

11

Nickie looked up and down the fluorescent-lit hallway lined with lockers that led from the meeting room to the shower stalls. The clanging of locker doors had stopped to be replaced by a dozen steamy showers hissing in unison. Turning her recorder off, she noted that she had little tape left. Thinking that his shower—since she had not yet set eyes on him—was probably the longest in the annals of baseball history, she had prepared to zing him a question that would pack the biggest wallop in the fewest possible words. There was, she checked, about a minute of tape left, and she knew that her listeners would rather hear Boone's voice than hers. She tapped her foot impatiently, an alluring figure in rose velvet jeans, black blouse, and vest. With her long legs, slim hips, and full breasts, Nickie had no trouble at all with clothes. Though she had long ago adopted her own northwestern style of Greenwich Village chic, she had often been told by envious acquaintances that she would look good even in Woolworth's off the rack. Comfortable in her sometimes zany, often elegant choice of attire Nickie seldom paid much attention to the dictates of the fashion industry. It was a rare occasion that would induce her to put on a dress in some swirly, feminine fabric.

Fearing that she looked like someone waiting for a bus, she put down her cassette and microphone and began shuffling through her notes in order to rehearse her end of the interview. She was glad she was on the interrogating end of this session for she knew her questions were rough. As the minutes ticked by and the other players sauntered back from the showers paying her scarcely any more heed, Nickie began to wonder if Craig Boone was ever going to show up. Had that big lunk passed out in the shower or had he made a hasty escape through a bathroom window?

At the thought that she might not get this coveted interview, beads of perspiration stood out on her forehead. Without Craig Boone, her piece would be lackluster at best. His was the name which made women take an unaccustomed interest in baseball and men stay glued to their radios or television sets for every Vikings game he pitched. He was a phenomenon in pitching. Hitters found him impossible to time and opposing pitchers found him impossible to imitate. Personally, Nickie found sports heroes, and heroes of any kind in fact, farcical. It was commendable that whatever they did was well done, but Craig Boone and all the other greats put on their shoes and socks in the morning just like the rest of the world. She could not understand people who went haywire at the sight of celebrities. She herself found their enormous egos boring, but the game they played fascinating. Her interest in Craig Boone was motivated solely by a drive to succeed. She would give her audience what they desired.

Though the warm dampness of the locker matted her curls against the back of her neck and her calves began to ache with all the foot tapping, her vigilance finally paid off. Craig Boone, with only a white Turkish towel wrapped around his lower torso, finally emerged from the showers. Why, as she gazed mesmerized at the tall, hulking form at the other end of the corridor, her heart began to race and her knees to shake she could not tell. The other players had been no more modestly attired. But, she answered herself wryly, the other players did not have quite the same physique to cover. Craig Boone was a big man. Black hair curled richly over a broad chest and tautly muscled abdomen. Sinewy veins bulged in tanned arms that looked to her stunned eyes more powerful than Goliath's. Having no idea how powerful Goliath had been, Nickie thought, in a split-second's amused lucidity, that was a perfectly acceptable simile. Boone was obviously not photogenic. On the screen or even from the stands he looked attractive but not more than that. In real life his eyes managed to convey an oddly mismatched and disturbing array of qualities. They formed at once deep brown pools that mirrored a gentleness of soul, a hard glint that promised an iron will, and a subdued twinkle that hinted at wit. Blue-black unstylishly long hair waved over his ears to surround a face that was both rugged for its square jaw and sensitive for its prominent cheekbones. Craig Boone's looks were a mass of contradictions. Nickie reminded herself sternly that his personality could certainly not match his looks for interest.

As Boone caught sight of Nickie from fifty feet away, he hesitated before continuing in his loping strides toward her. Their eyes locked for a microsecond's dizzying sensation before Boone looked away.

"Mr. Boone," Nickie called clearly as he came within earshot. "I'd like to ask you a few questions. Picking up her mike and pulling it hastily from its cover, she thrust it forward. Without pausing, Boone's eyes traveled insolently from her face to her toes, resting slightly too long at the place where her black silk blouse spread open against her creamy white skin.

Unaccustomed to the tingling effect of his eyes upon her, Nickie blushed furiously.

"About the St. Louis game tomorrow, our fans out there want to know . . ."

"I don't talk to reporters," Boone interrupted with quiet authority. "Especially when they barge in where they're not supposed to be."

"But, Mr. Boone!" Nickie stepped into his path.

14

Without changing his stride, Craig Boone jostled past her, causing her notebook, purse, and pen to fly out of her hands and scatter on the cement floor. She struggled clumsily off-balance to hold on to the tape recorder and mike. Looks certainly are deceiving, she thought furiously as she raised her eyes to glare at his retreating form. Her eyes met his twinkling orbs again as he looked back. Only this time they seemed to be laughing at her. Nickie bit her tongue. It wouldn't do, as was her wont, to yell after him that he was a jerk! She would get him better than that, she decided. Tomorrow she was to be given the opportunity to broadcast part of the big game against St. Louis. His pitching had better be faultless, because her audience would hear about every little error that Mr. Great was bound to make!

As she got from her knees to her feet, she prayed that nobody would bear witness to the way she scurried, like a mouse with its tail between its legs, out of the clubhouse.

CHAPTER TWO

When the alarm rang at six thirty the next morning, it seemed to Nickie that she had only just drifted off. Reaching out her arm to silence the infernal buzzing, she curled sleepily under her down quilt, which she slept with no matter what the season. At least let her finish that nice dream. As too often happens with nice dreams, she couldn't remember it, and its glow was fading. All she remembered was that a man figured in it.

A little later, as she got her breakfast of coffee and toast ready in the cooking nook of her studio apartment, Nickie gazed out the wide expanse of window on either side of the room. From the western exposure she beheld the snow-capped Olympic mountains and from the southern she could see majestic Mount Rainier. She had rented this flat at the northern tip of Seattle near Point Defiance Park, even though it was inconveniently located and small, solely because of the breathtaking view. For her, the vista before her was worth every penny it cost even though it just about decimated her pay check. Friends had clucked their tongues or shaken their heads in disbelief, for in truth the apartment offered little more in the way of amenities than scenery. The appliances were old, the plumbing roared, and the plaster was chipping. Nickie would not have noticed these things had it not been for the goodness of her friends, who willingly pointed them out. Though she saw them now, they didn't bother her. She concentrated more on the splendid red of her coleus plant than on the rust stain in her sink.

Having sipped the last drop of gourmet Colombian coffee—one of the few luxuries in which she regularly indulged—Nickie hurriedly dressed. As she absentmindedly picked the lint from her yellow lamb's wool sweater with the cowl neck and her umber knickers, she reviewed the day's agenda. She had to transcribe yesterday's taping for the files (her station unfortunately was short on secretarial help), and line up questions for today's game in case her mind played tricks and went numb just as she had a coach at the ready. That had never happened to her, but she had heard stories about just such an event befalling some of the most experienced broadcasters. She also had to get background information on the St. Louis team. All this before the game at two! And people thought her job was a cream puff, that she did nothing but get free seats for all the games!

Traffic was sparse on the way to the station, so she was able to gear up her snappy little Mazda sports coupe and arrive at the office at the same time as the office manager. Stan Metz was a dour-faced misogynist. That he had hired her reluctantly was obvious, for he did little to mask his dislike of her. Metz, like many of the others she dealt with, felt that women had no place in the man's world of sports. He was simply biding his time till he could justify firing her. He took no pains in keeping his plan from her. She would fail for she was a woman, he reasoned. And blast the temper of the times which had forced him to hire her in the first place.

17

"Alexander," he told her more than once, "you had better be out looking for a husband, going to dances and such, for pretty as you are you'll soon be wrinkled up like a prune and spend the rest of your life a spinster."

"I'm a reporter, Stan. I don't know the first thing about spinning. And don't you worry your head about it," she would mock in a fake southern accent. "Little ol' Nickie can take care of her own little life with or without the aid of any gentlemen callers, thank you."

"Say that with a smile at least," Stan growled in his best chauvinistic manner. The command caused Nickie's frown to deepen into a scowl.

What a way to start her day, she thought ruefully. With a mug of black coffee, she settled herself at her desk, cleared a space in the middle of the jumble, and commenced working. Scattered sheets of papers kept sliding from the pile at the front of her desk into her small clearing. Nickie made a silent promise to herself that she would clean up the mess and become more organized. Tomorrow. Interrupting for a moment her train of thought, Nickie took stock of herself. She was a hard worker, had guts, a certain amount of inspiration, and a good head. What she didn't have was a methodical nature. No one could accuse her of tidiness once they glanced in her silverware drawer at home or her file chest at work. She would change though, she solemnly promised herself. Too much time was being wasted in looking for things.

Quickly disposing of the typing and research she had to do, Nickie started planning her interview. She thought about each player in turn on both teams, about their strengths and weaknesses. She made up some sample questions. Of course she could not plan her interview entirely. Her questions would have to reflect the events of the game as they unfolded. The unpredictability of sports was one of the reasons she was attracted to the business. In almost every other situation one could guess with a certain reasonableness the outcome. Not so with sports. There was no canned laughter or violins tugging at your heartstrings to let you know what kind of ending to expect. So immersed was she in batting averages and errors that she was startled when the little travel alarm clock that she kept in front of her rang at one o'clock. After she had missed a game her first day at the job, she always set her clock to remind herself to get her nose out of her data. That first day's gaffe had really rankled. Besides the disappointment it was in its own right, she knew that it made Stan Metz happy, for wasn't she a typical woman, always late?

Grabbing her oversized shoulder bag, she rushed out of the office. She disliked going anywhere without that bag, though it looked disreputably worn with its cracked and faded leather. A gift from her uncle Ned, it brought her luck, she was certain. She refused Stan's offer of a lift to the stadium. Driving calmed her down and helped her to collect her thoughts. Her thoughts, she hated to admit, were not only of baseball. There was a stretch of about four green lights where she daydreamed of inheriting Howard Cosell's spot in sports. How she would love to be the woman whom all America loved to hate! Aware that to many people an ambitious woman was considered a crazy woman, Nickie kept her dreams to herself. She considered herself perfectly normal. And, she often thought, taking her background into account, she was a picture of mental health. Nickie's parents had died when she was ten. Her adored father, a flying buff, had been trying to teach her scatterbrained mother to fly his new Cessna. Somehow she had messed up, causing the two of them to fall to a fiery death. Nickie had never gotten all the details of the crash. Somehow it didn't seem to matter. In her ten-year-old mind her life had been numbed with sadness and pain—and an overwhelming sense of being alone.

The matter of who was going to keep Nickie had been clandestinely decided. Not privy to the council of her elders, she tried vainly to shut out the harsh whispers and hastily invented excuses of why her three aunts, all with children of their own, could not take her. Sibling rivalry was a term she heard often, though she knew not what it meant. A disruption of the family unit was another phrase. Well, let them put her in an orphanage! She didn't care. Without her parents there was nothing for her anyhow. The most she could hope for, she thought in a young, inarticulate way, was a lack of physical abuse. Her aunts were not thinking of her. They were thinking of themselves and of the inconvenience she would pose to them. They didn't understand Nickie as they had never understood her parents. Partisans of the school of split-level homes and Danish contemporary furniture, her aunts could never comprehend that some people preferred to spend their money on books or puppet shows and long vacations in the lake country.

Her aunts considered Nickie a strange child, and she knew that they found her dry eyes through the funeral and its aftermath distasteful. They didn't see that Nickie's heart was so broken to bits that she was beyond tears. And since they didn't change her pillowcase, leaving it to the child, they never found it stiff in the morning from sobs muffled by feathers and unleashed by sleep.

Just as things were coming to an impasse between her aunts, Nickie was saved by the arrival of her father's two bachelor brothers, Ned and Zak. Ned, the youngest of the

20

three brothers, was a handsome, devil-may-care wheeler-dealer. He had never gotten serious about life. Zak, the eldest, had a small muffler business in southern Florida, where he spent much of his time chasing rich widows. Ned and Zak saw to the tormented depths of little Nickie's soul immediately. And in less time than it took to unpack their bags they informed the terror-stricken child that she would live with them. Through a solicitor, Zak sold his business in Florida and Ned tied up the unfinished ends of whatever he happened to be into. Together they looked for a small house and Nickie's opinion was carefully considered. Since she was the only female in the new household her opinion on most household matters was quite seriously taken into account.

Uncle Ned and Uncle Zak tried hard to make up to her for her loss. They took her to movies, taught her to play ball, and one year when she was in sixth grade Uncle Ned even became class mother. Nickie's grief slowly attenuated and in a little more than a year they had her laughing again. Even today, eighteen years later, with Uncle Zak back in Florida and Uncle Ned galavanting around somewhere, her throat would constrict to think that two such unlikely fellows would give up their own lives for a little girl whom they had only seen perhaps two dozen times before.

Although her unorthodox upbringing had been lacking in some of the finer points, such as what colors matched and how a girl should sit with ankles crossed, Nickie did learn to throw a mean fast ball, score a touchdown, and fly cast. She also learned that the world could be a topsy-turvy place, and if you wanted to land upright, your feet had better be firmly planted in the ground. You had to be able to count on yourself. It was all anyone really had.

Once, when she was twenty years old, Nickie had fallen madly in love with a young man, an anthropology graduate student at the University of Washington. She was ready to settle down to home and garden when her young paramour decided that his career was more important than his love life and the two were mutually exclusive. He summarily informed her that in his upcoming field work in the wilds of New Guinea or outer Mongolia or Hoboken, a wife would be a major hindrance.

"Have a nice life, Nickie," were his parting words.

Nickie was a fast learner and having lost the two men in her life to whom she had been vulnerable, her father and her fiancé, she decided that men were for her, from that moment on, a species to approach with caution.

The parking attendants at the baseball stadium recognized Nickie as she entered the gates and waved her on to VIP parking. That was nice treatment for a member of the press. She flashed them a grateful smile for the shorter distance she would have to lug her paraphernalia. She could have allowed Stan Metz to bring down her recording equipment, but she felt more secure knowing she had it safely on her person.

She was going to have a five-minute spot on the five thirty and six o'clock news tonight to summarize the game, and she wanted everything to go perfectly. It was a coveted spot for the large number of listeners she would reach, a captive audience in the rush-hour traffic.

Settling down in the press box, she barely nodded to her coworkers. Her stomach was as nervous as if the outcome of the game depended on her, she thought disgustedly. As the first inning began, she forgot herself and became immersed in baseball. She even forgot to find fault with Craig Boone. The game was a close one but happily Seattle came out victorious. She hastily jotted down the chronology of events as the audio technicians surrounded her for the recording. She looked smaller than she was, standing knee deep in equipment with technicians running to and fro as if they themselves were orchestrating a World Series.

She counted to herself as the assistant signaled that they were ready. The red recording light was on. And Nickie delivered. She ended by saying, "And that's the way it was, folks, this afternoon at Three Rivers Stadium with our Vikings pulling it out in the ninth inning by a score of three to two. Back to you, Ted."

"That was okay, Alexander," Stan called out grudgingly. Wiping her brow Nickie acknowledged the compliment with a nod.

Reassembling her notes, she bent to pick up her bag when an odd almost imperceptible sensation at the back of her neck made her turn around. There was Craig Boone leaning on his bat, staring straight at her. He wore a funny, sardonic grin. Plucking up her courage, despite the goose bumps on her arms, Nickie walked determinedly in his direction. Though he was a boor and she had no desire for a repeat performance of yesterday's scene, she concentrated on Howard Cosell. If her name was to be a household word someday like Cosell's, then she would have to put up with all sorts of things, including the likes of Craig Boone.

"Mr. Boone," she called out in a quavery voice, "what pitch did you use in the eighth to strike out Kozenski?" Without waiting for an answer and scarcely pausing for breath she followed up, "And by the way, is your arm responding to the new whirlpool treatment?"

Boone's grin became wider. "Who fed you those questions, girl?"

23

"My name's not girl and those are my questions."

"What is your name then?"

"Sophia Loren. Now about your arm?"

"I'll tell you all about my arm and maybe even demonstrate my curve ball if you come to my apartment around nine." He smirked. "I'm in the white pages."

Nickie felt the blood drain from her face. "I won't dignify that with a response, Mr. Boone." She turned on her heel and marched indignantly back to her seat, where she collected the rest of her gear. She heard footsteps behind her. A hand reached out to her elbow.

"Hey, I'm sorry. That was a pretty awful thing to say."

She shook her arm free. "That's quite all right, Mr. Boone." Swallowing convulsively she took a deep breath. "Let's get back to that pitch in the eighth . . ."

Boone studied her for a long moment, and with his big, luminescent eyes twinkling, he answered seriously. "I used a screwball to get Kozenski. Normally I wouldn't use a trick pitch; it's bad for the arm, but I had the idea that Kozenski was getting a feel for my timing. The kid needed a jolt; he needed to know there were some tricks I could pull out of the bag if I wanted. And as for my arm, well, that's coming along with the mineral baths I'm using. The salts are sent to me from the Dead Sea in Israel. They really can't be beat. Of course I wouldn't be having this problem with my arm if I stayed on a five-day rotation, but it's the middle of the season, and they need me out there, sometimes every three or four days. If it'll get us into the playoffs, I'm willing to do my part."

Having neglected to set up her recording equipment, Nickie was furiously scribbling in an illegible shorthand which was a combination of high school learned, forgotten Pitman and her own brand of speedwriting. She often

24

joked to the receptionist at the station that if she were a spy the Russians could never crack her code.

She looked up to ask him what he thought of the new club owner. The intensity of his gaze upon her face made her hesitate and caused her to lose her advantage.

"You're quite an enigma," he drawled. "Did anybody ever ask you what a . . ."

"Nice girl like me is doing in a profession like this?" she cut in. "Many a time. Quite frankly, I'm tired of it."

"Whoa, don't jump to conclusions. That's not what I was going to say."

"Oh," she said in a small voice.

Craig Boone smiled. "You've got a lot to learn. You need a good teacher."

"Are you volunteering your services?" she asked acidly.

"You wouldn't pay for them, would you?" Boone laughed.

"This is getting out of hand," Nickie replied. "Thank you for the interview." She picked up her bag.

"Wait a minute! You haven't told me your name."

"Nickie Alexander."

"Nickie," he repeated. "That sounds like it could be short for Nicole."

"That's right," she answered shortly.

"How about dinner tonight, Nicole?"

"You've got to be kidding," she fumed.

Craig Boone laughed. "Your high spirits lurk dangerously close to shrewishness. Lucky for you I can see to the warm, sensual woman beneath that artillery shell you have wrapped around you."

"Yechh!" she said with feeling. "Sounds like you watch the soaps on your days off. I think I may mention that on the air tonight."

Boone laughed out loud. Nothing could shake that man's equanimity.

"You can say what you want about me—as long as I get what I want. And I know what I want." His eyes flickered mirthfully over her body.

To her dismay, Nickie felt a warm, unaccustomed sensation stirring deep within her.

"Mr. Boone, the interview is over."

"The name's Craig, Nicole. I'll meet you at the Café de la Paix at eight. The table will be reserved."

"The name's Nickie, not Nicole, and the answer is an unequivocal no!" Nickie shook her head for emphasis and with full arms practically ran to her car.

Back at the station she successfully implored Stan Metz to give her an extra minute of air time at the end of her taped segment, so she could relate the items she had gotten from Boone. Almost every other bit of personal information about him was matter of public record, so she was sure that his broken reserve would be a matter of speculation in newsy circles. The technicians didn't want to splice the tape, so her addition would be done live. Nickie preferred a pretaping, because she always feared that she would sneeze or hiccup on the air.

It was seven o'clock by the time Nickie left the station and all had gone well. As she started the ignition of her car, the unwelcome thought that she was less than a mile from the Café de la Paix entered her consciousness. She paused before stepping on the gas and nosing her vehicle firmly in the opposite direction.

The nerve of him to think that she would show up at a restaurant after the way he had spoken to her! Of course she might be able to get some unparalleled scoops. She banished the thought. Was he a meat-and-potatoes man?

Probably. She reprimanded her wayward mind once more. She most certainly didn't want the opportunity to find out!

At home finally, Nickie just had the energy to take a small crab quiche out of her freezer and pop it in her toaster oven. She had made it the previous weekend and had frozen it for just such an evening after a hard day's work. Though she lived alone, Nickie enjoyed cooking and often tried out new recipes. She didn't feel that because she wasn't cooking for an army or a husband she should deny herself the pleasure of good eating and live on commercial frozen food, even if it did come in attractive packaging these days and call itself by French names. Supermarket frozen food was supermarket frozen food no matter which way you pronounced it.

Nickie sank down in the corduroy recliner that faced the mountains and tried to relax. It was eight o'clock now. She would have been giving the maître d' her name and allowing him to bow and scrape as he led her to Craig Boone's table. Craig would rise in greeting, smile graciously, and ask if he could pour her a glass of champagne from the bottle of imported stuff sitting in the gold-etched ice bucket. He would regale her with amusing stories and tend to her unspoken whims.

If only fantasies could be so sweetly realized! What would have been more likely had she made the mistake of accepting his invitation, or his command, was that he would have offered her a beer and insulted her with vulgar sexual innuendos in between mouthfuls of tenderloin. It was a good thing that she had common sense. Many a woman in her position would have only too easily allowed themselves to be swept off their feet by proximity to a sports super star. Especially one who was so handsome and had such penetrating eyes and gave a woman the

27

feeling that he could command her the way he could command a ball nestled in his big hand. No one would ever dominate Nickie Alexander. She was the master of her own destiny.

The phone pierced her reverie, making her jump. She ran to answer it, but with hand a mere inch from the receiver, she stopped. It was probably Craig, and what was there to say? She wouldn't allow herself to be convinced to come, nor to be reprimanded for staying home. Better to ignore the rings. Yet each of its eight blasts sounded like an arrow in her gut. The phone rang again later that night and then once more. Each time, Nickie steeled herself against answering it. She fell asleep with a book of short stories by her side, still opened to page one.

CHAPTER THREE

The next day Nickie put baseball out of her head. The women's regional softball playoffs were to be held in Olympia, and she was going to be there. A small measure of independence was hers in this job as long as she made sure to cover major sporting events. Reporters usually did in-depth reports about Major Leagues when there was no game to cover. Nickie, however, conceived a broader picture of sports, which she hoped to impart to her listeners and, if she were lucky, to the sports establishment. She felt that sports should be for everyone, and that meant women as well as men. There was a lot going on that no one cared much about, and women's softball was one example.

As she expected, she was the only media person covering the game. The women on the four playoff teams greeted her warmly. They asked her into the dugout, gave her a cup of iced tea, vied with each other for a chance to give her whatever information they thought she would need. It was a reception far different from that accorded her by men's baseball.

In years past Nickie had attended a few of these softball games as a spectator rather than as a reporter. Although she preferred to play baseball, she was inevitably impressed by the skill and dedication of these players. This was not a big-money sport. The women, in fact, had to pay their own travel expenses. It was purely a labor of love for them.

Even now, sitting on the edge of her seat, she was astounded at the pitchers' strength. It was not unusual for these women to throw balls which reached speeds of eighty miles an hour, no mean feat considering that in softball the throw was underhand and the ball bigger and softer than in baseball. So intrigued with events in front of her, Nickie forgot all about taking notes. It didn't matter, she decided, as she realized her negligence. If only she could convey to her listeners the excitement, the fast action, and the passion of this sport, she would be doing it a far greater service than merely reporting wins and losses. The flavor of the game could be captured as much in the emotional aftermath as the winning team broke out in whoops, screams, and kisses, and the losing teams in tears, as in a recording of the events on the field. It seemed to her that these players cared more about their game than some pros. This was the thrill of a sport in its purest sense. She wondered amusedly how the Seattle Vikings would make out against the Amazons of Olympia.

She felt a glow on the ride back to Seattle. Seeing a sport played like that, for sheer joy, was gratifying. The picture of softball which she gave on the news that night was electrifying in its emotional tone. Nickie barred no holds, but told her listeners exactly how that game today made her feel; like a kid with a first ball park hotdog. There were no managers cursing the umps, no team players publicly bawling out players for error, no tight-lipped, grim-faced players. There was a group of women with every face mirroring an entire gauntlet of emotions, as visions of victory appeared and disappeared. Nickie appealed to her

30

listeners to participate themselves in a sport and to find an amateur club to root for and to sponsor.

"Let's have a sports renaissance, folks. Big-time sports are great but so are little-time sports. Let's not take the excitement and challenge of competitive play away from the people. It belongs to you! This is Nickie Alexander wishing you a good night and good playing."

Squaring her shoulders, Nickie pressed the off button on her mike. She was proud of herself, and she knew that her uncles Ned and Zak would have been too, had they heard her tonight. It was they who had instilled in her a love for games, well and lustily played.

She was not too late, as she left the recording room, to hear ribald laughter coming from Stan Metz and the two technicians working with him.

"Next thing she'll be doing is pigeon fighting," one of them cracked.

"Yeah, or maybe a special on women bull fighters," another rejoined.

"Guys, she'll have the scoop on the tiddlywinks championship, or I'll eat my hat," Metz said, and cackled.

Nickie froze without uttering a sound till Metz noticed her. Without referring to what she'd overheard, nor exhibiting any signs of unease, he told her to help Ruthanne, the receptionist and Girl Friday, with next week's programming schedules. Frowning at the three men, Nickie went into the outer office where Ruthanne had her desk. This wasn't a part of her job, she knew, and not at all what she had signed up for. Considering what she had just heard, she really ought to stomp out and head home. But Ruthanne was a friend, a warm, sincere, motherly woman who was burdened with even more diffuse duties than Nickie herself. Her title should have been efficiency expert, financial wizard, and Queen of WRPJ, Nickie often joked. More to help Ruthanne out than to acquiesce to Metz's request Nickie did as she was asked. Maybe if they worked together they could get out of here at a reasonable hour.

"I heard what went on out there," Ruthanne said sympathetically. "Don't you worry about it. You did real well, and I think those macho men know it too," she said with a wink.

Shaking her shoulders dejectedly, Nickie looked fondly at the plump wrinkled face of her friend. "Do you really think I was okay?"

"I won't say you weren't controversial," Ruthanne said seriously, "but that's what a station needs to up its ratings. I personally agreed with everything you said, though I think you'll get some flak for it. But you know that, and you know it's going to be a long, hard climb."

"Yes, of course." Nickie sighed. "Though sometimes when I hear my name bandied about, I wish I could have been satisfied teaching in a junior high school. Well, I guess it's true that anything worthwhile isn't going to come easy. I'm going to be up there with the best of them. And this isn't just a pipe dream."

"Why don't you go on home," Ruthanne said gently. "You look a little piqued and tomorrow is the big game at Lincoln Park against WORQ. You'll be playing, won't you?"

"Oh, my gosh, I forgot all about that. Tomorrow! And I'm playing short stop. I wonder if WORQ is going to have any women playing."

"I don't know, but I'll tell you one thing. You'd better be well rested if you're going to do us proud. And yourself proud. Some of the Vikings are going to be on hand to umpire and cheer."

"Was that publicity gimmick the brainchild of Stan Metz?" Nickie asked dryly.

"Who else? He's a little short on personality, but he's a born ad man."

"Craig Boone won't be there, will he?" Nickie asked a little too offhandedly.

"I doubt it. Why? Are you interested in him?" Ruthanne asked suspiciously.

"No, of course not. I never mix business with pleasure."

"Too bad, since you come in contact with so many gorgeous, rich men."

"I've learned the hard way that gorgeous and rich aren't necessarily what I'm looking for."

"If it's ugly and poor you're after that shouldn't be too hard to find."

"What I'm really after"—Nickie chuckled—"is a good, kind, sensitive, strong liberated man who will not only do the dinner dishes but also the dinner, replete with fabulous soufflé and centerpiece, and then support me unflinchingly in all my endeavors. Athletes are too wrapped up in themselves."

"Dream on, girl!" Ruthanne chortled. "Meanwhile, did I ever tell you about my nephew, the optometrist?"

"Only fifty times, as well as about the dentist's son who lives down the street and the accountant who does your tax returns and got divorced last year."

"You can't blame me for trying," Ruthanne said and sighed. "There's nothing I'd rather see than you wearing an apron and rocking a bassinet."

"There's lots of ways to be happy. I'd like to see myself on national television doing a World Series play by play."

"My poor dear child," Ruthanne chided sympathetically, "I know you're joking about your dream man, but I also sense that marriage doesn't rank very high on your list of priorities. I only hope that whatever happened in your young life to so turn you into yourself can be undone. I hope the right man comes along to do it."

Nickie felt a tightening in her chest. She didn't reply right away.

"I'll let you know if Mr. Right comes knocking at my door. C'mon, let's get this work done."

On her way home that night she mulled over Ruthanne's words. Her friend, the mother of four grown children, meant well but could see no ultimate destiny for a woman other than the traditional one of wife and mother. Nickie put her musings to rest. Ruthanne did not have a modern attitude toward life.

CHAPTER FOUR

The day of the game dawned sunny and bright. The air was musky with the winesap smells of late summer. Wearing a burgundy sweatsuit, Nickie arrived early at Lincoln Park in order to warm up. As she breathed the honeyed fragrance of clover and wild roses, she felt heady with anticipation. Playing baseball was one of her favorite things in the world. She loved the sound of her bat as it cracked firmly against the ball; she loved the feel of the hard-packed dirt under her feet as she ran swiftly around the bases and, she was forced to admit to herself, she loved the stunned faces of onlookers as they watched this slender woman playing like a champ.

She bent from the waist to touch her toes, stretched her legs in back of her, and bounced to stretch her tendons. She finished her exercises with her customary twenty push-ups. She stood on her tiptoes, reaching high, her arms toward the trees. The cloudless blue of the sky against the netting of branches made her thankful that she had eyes to see and the sense to use them. She started running along the beach which bordered Puget Sound. Not wanting to tire herself out, she decided that she would only do two miles. That meant hardly enough time to work up a sweat and nowhere near enough running to reach the euphoria where all pain disappeared and running became a dream. She had the scenery all to herself save for a family of mallards which were swimming lazily in circles and for one canoist who waved at her in the friendly, unselfconscious style of fellow travelers.

As she finished her run, Nickie sat for some minutes on a grassy knoll overlooking the sound. She rose as she heard the voices of the first players to arrive. The D.J.s, newscasters, and sportscasters of Seattle's two major rival stations had planned this game for several weeks. It was publicized in a light, joking vein, but Nickie knew that each team was desperate to win. It had taken some demonstrating of her skills and not a little convincing to secure the position of shortstop for herself. Stan Metz had grudgingly agreed, figuring shrewdly that if they lost, they could blame the loss on their egalitarian stance in having given a key position to a woman.

It was half an hour to game time. Nickie took a pair of heavy knit white socks out of her canvas bag and the roll of white surgical tape, which she would use to tape the socks below her knees, so they would not fall down or bunch up while she was running the bases.

Decked out in traditional baseball garb, looking anything but glamorous, Nickie sauntered over to the diamond. It was well kept, with emerald-green grass and smooth dirt carefully packed at the pitcher's mound. She was greeted by the other station's players.

"Hey, Nickie, you gonna knock us dead today?" called a weatherman.

"Not dead," she yelled back from where she was standing at the bleachers. "Just unconscious!"

"How'd ya ever get Metz to let you play?" jeered a sound engineer. "He doesn't like losing."

Knucklehead! Nickie thought to herself, deciding to ignore the barb. She was relieved to hear the crew from WRPJ arriving. They weren't great, but at least they wouldn't say that stuff to her face. All of a sudden Nickie felt a pervading loneliness. It wasn't easy being a female in an all-male environment.

She was glad to see that most of the wives had come along to root for the team, and of course Ruthanne was there with her husband and her two youngest children. She walked over to meet them. Metz was the self-appointed manager, and as such was talking to the players in a voice gruffer than was natural for him.

"And you . . ." He turned to face Nickie. "You've been telling me what you're made of from the first time I laid eyes on you. Today you'd better prove it!"

As Nickie walked up to the plate at the bottom of the second with two players out, she remembered that exhortation. She was going to really show that Stan Metz.

"Come on, Nickie, hit it. Let's go, girl!"

Looking fragile yet determined, she swung her oversized bat menacingly, unaware of the noise from the bleachers. Her uncles were great baseball fans, and she had played all her life. From childhood on, each time she came up to bat she would neither see nor hear anything except the ball and the bat.

Mort Grimes, a middle-aged editorialist for the rival station, threw her a beautiful slow pitch right over the plate. With a shallow intake of breath, Nickie tightened up and swung solidly, lining the ball between the left and center fielders. The crowd roared as Nickie flew over the bases to stand grinning on third base with a triple by the time the ball was returned. The next player got a single, and Nickie ran home amidst cheers to make the first run of the game. She was greeted with backslaps, congratulations, and a beer, which she refused in favor of a Coke. During the next six innings she made three more hits and fielded flawlessly with the leaping catches which had earned her the affectionate nickname of Frog from her uncles. She had noticed some of the Vikings in the stands and for their benefit as much as for her own had outperformed herself. If she was going to be covering them for the station, they ought to at least respect her, and after today she was sure they would.

It wasn't until the last inning of the game that she saw Craig Boone. She was out in the field playing shortstop when she caught sight of him smiling at her from behind the foul line.

It looks as if he's just arrived, she thought to herself, angry at the way her mouth had gone suddenly dry and her heart palpitated. Just then a slow, easy, high-bouncing ground ball came her way. With fingers unusually slippery inside her well-worn glove she caught it, fumbled, got hold of it again, dropped it, and finally picked it up to throw it wildly past the first baseman. The crowd, which had loved her for eight innings, responded with boos. Red-faced and chagrined for playing "just like a girl," Nickie glanced surreptitiously up from her feet to check the foul line. Craig Boone hadn't moved, but the grin on his face had gotten wider. Nickie bit her lip and prayed that no more balls would come her way this inning because she could feel herself shaking. An error such as she had just made was quite unnerving.

The game ended with a four–three victory for WRPJ. Though she knew she should be rejoicing with her teammates, who were running all over the field, the fact that her last play had been a bad one put a damper on her spirits. Dragging her heels and kicking her toes into the cool earth, she walked back to the dugout. Even as she noticed the big shadow looming over her she cast her eyes determinedly on her cleated feet.

"Anybody can make an error," Craig Boone said softly. Nickie swallowed the lump which had appeared in her throat.

"I played well before you came." *Why did I have to say that?* she shrieked inwardly, barely controlling an urge to kick herself.

"I don't doubt that you did," he replied. "Any number of people," he gestured toward the stands, "are discussing your exploits play by play."

Nickie wiped her flushed face with the back of her hand. Craig offered her his large white handkerchief, which she took gratefully.

"What are you doing here?" She was anxious to change the topic. "You generally avoid publicity stunts."

"True, but I like baseball . . . of all sorts," he added with a smirk. "And I like you."

"You don't even know me. And it seems that you think I'm some sort of combination battle-ax and virago."

"On the contrary." He laughed. "I think you're exciting, not to mention interesting. You might be a smidgeon too ambitious, but we can work on that."

"*We*'re not going to work on anything. I'm very happy the way I am."

"Can't we even work on lunch?" His smile was winsome. "After that workout I'll bet you could use some nourishment."

"I brought a sandwich with me."

"Feed it to the pigeons. Let me take you to a superb little French restaurant I know. It's *splendide . . . mag-*

nifique . . . for two ballplayers like us," he said, and winked.

"Well." She hesitated. Her mind worked furiously. He was terribly attractive. But she was sure he only saw her as a challenge, a proving ground for his male ego. But then, she rationalized, he might provide some useful information for her broadcasts, and goodness knows, no man would ever let foolish pride stand in the way of an opportunity like this. And the price of the lunch wouldn't even make a dent in his wallet.

"How about it?" he broke into her thoughts. "I don't bite."

"All right. But"—she looked at her watch—"I can't stay too long. Saturday is my day for chores."

"I'll get you home way before the witching hour, Cinderella."

"Can I go dressed like this?" She pointed to her rumpled sweat suit.

"Don't worry about it. You're with me." He took her arm by the elbow and guided her to his car, a cream-colored Maserati the likes of which Nickie had only seen in glossy advertisements in the slickest of magazines. She turned around to see if her encounter with Boone had been observed by anyone. Ruthanne was watching her concentratedly, and as her friend caught Nickie's eye, she clasped both hands over her head in a victory wave. Nickie grimaced, though she doubted Ruthanne could see the expression on her face from that distance.

"That's a nice car you have."

"I like beautiful things." He flashed her a bemused smile. Shrugging to show her annoyance, Nickie thought that she might do well to retract her acceptance of this luncheon. Having come to think of her striking good looks

40

as more of a hindrance in business than a help, she didn't, at this point, want to be judged on how she looked, but rather on what she was.

"I suppose with your obscene salary you can afford beautiful things," she answered dryly.

"I'm not an especially big spender. I indulge myself rarely. Most of my money is tied up in business endeavors and in various other things."

"Oh?" Nickie's interest was piqued. "What sort of business endeavors?"

"I've a small home computer company. It's the wave of the future and, well"—he laughed a little self-consciously—"I've always enjoyed mathematics."

"Computers and baseball, hmmm. What do you do, program yourself to win?"

"Would that I could." He laughed.

"That's quite a big chunk you've bitten off."

"It keeps me out of trouble, even if it does give me indigestion at times."

Comfortably ensconced in the soft leather seats, Nickie watched as he handled the car with an easy expertise. With all its luminous dials the dashboard looked to her as if it belonged more in an airplane than in a car. He took his eyes momentarily from the road to smile directly at her.

"And what about those various other things you mentioned, Mr. Boone?"

"Craig."

"Okay, Craig."

"I don't talk about those other things, not even to you."

"I see." Nickie flushed, unable to censor the thought that those other things were probably a couple of mistresses he kept, nubile young things willing and eager to pleasure him in between his running to the clubhouse and his computer center. The thought that this was a business lunch could not console her for having come with him, for this was a man of apparently immense wealth who moved in a world she knew nothing of. The idea of being out of her depth made her ill at ease.

"Tell me about yourself, Nicole."

"There's not much to tell." She thought it surprising that she didn't mind his calling her Nicole.

"How did you get to be such a good ballplayer?"

"Lots of women are."

"Maybe, but not women who look like you."

"I've played most of my life. My uncles taught me when I was a child and coached me practically every day after I learned to swing a bat."

"They must have lived near you."

"You might say that. They brought me up. My parents were killed in a plane crash when I was ten."

"I'm sorry."

"Don't be. Everybody had to learn about life and death and hard knocks sooner or later. I learned sooner. Anyway Zak and Ned, my uncles, were good to me. They went to school on parents' night and sold Girl Scout cookies with me. They did what they could and even what they couldn't."

Nickie stopped short. She hadn't meant to tell him all that, and she hated the pitying look in his eye. She shook her head defiantly.

"I'm a lot better off than most people. I have no illusions about life. And I know what I am and what I can be."

"You must have some illusions left. I'm sure you do."

42

He looked thoughtful. "I'd like to meet your uncles. They sound like nice guys."

"I rarely see them," she said a little sadly. "Zak is in Florida and Ned, well, I think he's in Colorado now. Since I reached the age of consent—I mean my majority—" she said, and gulped, "we get together two or three times a year—for Christmas, my birthday, and maybe for a World Series game if we like the teams."

As she talked, the Maserati was nosing soundlessly along Puget Sound and over the floating bridge on Lake Washington. A low-key city, without the flash of its California cousin, San Francisco, Seattle with its surrounding mountain ranges, its gently sloping hills, its unique skyline featuring the Space Needle, and its quaint shops, always succeeded in casting its spell over her. Its mood was relaxed, its song a Brahms lullaby.

Almost without realizing it, they arrived at the restaurant. The Canlis was one of those places which most of the people Nickie knew talked about in two ways; falsely, pretending to have dined there, or wistfully, aware that they could never afford to do so.

As a gold-liveried doorman with a Roman nose, haughty demeanor, and slightly cocked eyebrow opened the door, Nickie knew that she could not go in there dressed as she was even if she were escorted by the Prince of Wales. She twisted in her seat to prevent the doorman from hearing.

"Craig, I really don't think . . ."

Catching the discomfiture of her expression, Craig quickly rallied to her defense. "We're not here for lunch, Carl," he addressed the doorman with familiarity. "But I do have a request to make of Chef Boret." Motioning Carl to bend down, he whispered some instructions in his ear and unobtrusively slipped a bill into his palm.

"My pleasure, sir. I'll be back shortly."

Nickie looked questioningly at Craig, who answered simply, "It's far too nice a day to sit in a restaurant, even one with a superb view of Lake Union. In any case, one glance at you looking as if you were ready to be sick, and inspiration struck. I'm going to take you to a place that I've only taken two other people. But I'll tell you no more till we get there."

"Why the suspense?" Nickie asked in evident relief.

"It's more fun that way. The only thing that should be predictable is the weather."

"Is that why you're not married, to avoid the predictable?" She put her hand to her head. She shouldn't have asked that.

"I was married once. I'm divorced."

"I didn't know."

"How could you? I don't advertise the fact. My private life is private and my public life is baseball."

Nickie's curiosity was aroused and not only, she was loath to admit, on a professional level.

"Can I ask you a personal question?"

"Sure, that's the best kind."

"What happened? I mean why did you get a divorce?"

"You don't want to hear about Suzanne."

An illogical pang of jealousy struck Nickie as she heard him speak the name of his ex-wife.

"Why spoil a perfectly fine day?" he continued.

"I'm interested . . . Really I am."

"I guess you could say we were in-com-pat-ible." He drew out the word. "That's the current *à la mode* reason people give, isn't it? Or to be more specific Suzanne fancied herself an *artiste*." He gave the word a heavy Gallic inflection and laughed. "Suzanne thought she was a sculptor. She was forever pleading with me to pose for her. On the few occasions I agreed the end result looked more like Quasimodo than anything else. She claimed it was abstract. I claim it was lack of talent. To make a long, lurid story short, she used to drag me around to her "arty" friends' garrets and lofts. You might say I didn't quite fit in. They were the kind of people who smoked nonfiltered French cigarettes and thought it 'quaint' that I played baseball. My dear wife finally gave into the pressure and ran away with a Rumanian poet. The last I heard of her, a couple of years ago, she was married to a used car magnate." He laughed. "Now that's what I call poetic justice!"

"It sounds brutal," Nickie said sympathetically.

Craig was noncommittal. "It's over, ancient history. And what about you? Are you free, Nicole? Do you have a story? You must. I won't believe you don't have two or three stories, at the very least."

Nickie was spared the necessity of a response by the arrival of Carl. He was carrying a large straw basket, the kind you see in foreign films when a pair of lovers picnic, pants rolled up, at the seashore or in modern television beer commercials.

"Can you hold that on your lap?" Craig asked.

"No problem. I don't have to worry about wrinkling my outfit." Craig drove fast and didn't talk much. He skirted Seattle and headed for the outlying foothills. He took a narrow winding road, which would have had Nickie's pulse racing had she been the driver. The foliage on either side of them was lush, walling them in with greenery and muffling any sound. Nickie had to strain to make out even the soft hum of the motor.

"This is why I love living in Seattle." She gestured broadly to the verdant outdoors. A short drive and you can be in a rain forest or skiing in the mountains, and you still have the advantage of big-city culture and fascinating people."

"Thank you." He flashed a brilliant smile in her direction and gave a short laugh.

"I wasn't necessarily referring to you!" Nickie replied in a half-teasing tone.

"Weren't you?"

"And there are the disadvantages," she went on, as if she hadn't heard his question, "like the insufferable egotists one runs into at times."

"You've got spunk." He laughed, a deep, warm sound that had a strange effect on her. "That's refreshing. I get tired of the simpering violets and clinging vines I usually run into, not to mention the poisonous man-eating plants. I prefer my flowers in the garden."

"And I prefer mine wild on the sunny slope of an overgrown hill, or unexpected in a shady cove filled with driftwood."

"I would never think to find a poetic soul housed in the same body that can swing at a fast ball the way you're reputed to. It's a delightful combination; you're full of surprises."

"Anything to avoid predictability." She tried to squelch the smile that was tugging at the corners of her mouth.

"You do quite well at it. I used to think that there were two types of women: those that get ahead with their bodies and those that get ahead with their daddys. You're disabusing me of that notion."

"It's a notion you never should have had, not in this day and age. But if you want to be precise, I do get ahead with my body. It was my body that landed me on third base today my first time up."

"It was your mind that was the force behind that, your will." As Craig finished speaking, he swung the car sharply to his right and parked half in the deep undergrowth which was everywhere.

"We walk the rest of the way." He took the picnic basket from Nickie as he leaned over her to swing the door open. The air had a heavy rain forest quality to it that was lightened only by the sweet smell of flowers and herbs. Hibiscus mixed with cloying scent of gardenia and the feather-light hint of thyme to touch a chord of memory that Nickie never knew existed. Inexplicably she was filled with a longing and sadness that she could not name but which, as the mist nourished the grasses, nourished her soul. She looked at Craig's back as he led the way along the narrow thorn-spiked path, and the pantherlike roll of his shoulders and the sunlight playing off his black curls made her pulse quicken.

"Look at the blueberry bushes! Let's pick some." Her voice sounded, to her own ears, like a stranger's.

Without ado Craig put the picnic basket down, opened it, and brought out one of the plastic bags that the restaurant had thoughtfully provided for refuse.

"I don't know how good they'll be." He plucked a fat berry off the nearest bush to place on Nickie's lips. Never before had a blueberry made her lips tingle.

"Tart," she pronounced with an exaggerated pucker, "but fine for jams and jellies."

"Will you spread some on my breakfast toast?"

"I'll give you half of what I make, if I ever get around

to making it. And I'll wrap the jars with ribbons and bows," Nickie replied hastily.

She felt herself redden as she noticed that his eyes were laughing.

"A gentleman doesn't ask questions like that," she added finally. "But then again, you're not a gentleman."

"Since I'm no gentleman I'm not bound by the code of courtly conduct. And here I have you all alone in the woods. I could seduce you, or failing that, I could ravish you and no one would hear your cries of protest . . . or pleasure."

"You wouldn't." The dead calm of her voice did not betray a strange excitement stirring within her.

He laughed. "You're right. I only take what I'm given."

Nickie pursed her lips, amazed at the turn this conversation had taken. "I don't believe in giveaways."

Craig laughed again. "Let's pick those berries."

They worked silently side by side. Though it was a cool summer sun that shone, Nickie felt its heat upon her neck like the warm hand of a friend. She was calmer now, freer to enjoy this companionable, innocent pastime, that the moment of passion flickering behind the masks of banter and smiles had passed. When they had picked all of the plump berries, some with their skins bursting from the pale, juicy pulp, they filled their bag with small hard ones, tied the plastic in a knot, and feeling virtuous for the found diversion, headed for Craig's secret place and a lunch they were hungry for.

Having walked perhaps a quarter of a mile, they came to a bower where weeping willow trees hung like a diaphanous veil. Craig took her hand in his and led her through the trees, whose leaves caressed their faces like fairy fingers. On the other side was a grassy knoll that looked upon a sparkling waterfall as it fell into a creek.

"What a lovely spot!" Nickie gasped.

Craig nodded. "Some men take a shot of whiskey to make them feel good. I come here. Sit down." He patted the grass next to him and proceeded to unpack the lunch. First he laid down a white linen tablecloth. In the middle he placed a flat, wide-bottomed vase with a single long-stemmed rose. "Chef Boret thinks of everything." Next he set down the linen napkins and the real silver place settings and the crystal goblets.

Nickie sat cross-legged watching him in disbelief. "I'm afraid my style of picnic is more on the order of plastic cups, paper plates, and corned beef."

Wordlessly, Craig laid out the gold-rimmed Rosenthal china, popped the cork on Epernay's finest champagne, and toasted her with a flourish.

"You're a wild rose and your thorns cut deep at times, Nicole . . . but no flower is more desirable."

He clinked his glass to hers and took a long sip of the amber liquid. Without warning, his lips, still wet from champagne, were upon hers in a kiss so tender yet wanting that it could not but melt the cold place that she jealously guarded deep within her. As of its own volition her mouth answered his, probing, bruising, needing. Still sitting Indian-style, palms turned upward at her sides, neither touching nor being touched, save for this kiss, Nickie knew that what she was experiencing far surpassed the groping and grappling that most people regarded as intimacy. As suddenly as he began kissing her he ended. The taste of his champagne lingered upon her lips.

"Brut, extra dry," she said, hoping to deflect a reality she didn't care to further explore. She had worked too

49

hard to permit heartache to drag her down. Here was a man who was too aggressive, too domineering, too strong, not to wreck the course she had carefully plotted out for her life.

His eyes clouded over with a look she didn't understand. He opened the wrapped packages he had laid on the tablecloth.

"Homemade pâté de foie gras and the truffles are flown in from the South of France. Let's see what we have here." He unwrapped a porcelain seashell containing a dozen perfectly sculpted miniature butter shells. "*Voilà*, the bread." He held up a crusty baguette, the long French bread that makes France the spiritual home of bread lovers everywhere. "Cheese," Craig said on opening the next package. "Have you ever eaten *fromage du chèvre*, otherwise known as goat's cheese?"

Nickie shook her head. "I didn't know you spoke French."

"Only a little. Mainly I speak menu-ese."

He cut her a piece of pâté, a wedge of cheese, and the heel of the bread. The pâté was delicately flavored, smooth, and subtle along with the nutlike bouquet of the champagne. The white dry cheese was salted just slightly and somewhat gamy in flavor. Nickie enjoyed it for its uniqueness, but secretly thought that when it came to brown bagging she would stick to cheddar. Craig lay back on the grass, bread and pâté in hand, staring up at the cloudless sky. He placed his hand on her knee.

"This is the life." He lapsed into silence.

"Aren't you going to elaborate?" Nickie asked lightly.

"Are you fishing for compliments?"

"Why not?"

"All right," he acquiesced. "We've covered beauty and brains. Now we come to character."

Nickie laughed. "I have a better idea. I'll assess you. Looks—good to incredible." She paused. "Athletic prowess—one in a million. And now here's where you're unbeatable, the incomparable world's leading . . . con man! Don't think for a minute, Craig Boone, when you say all those nice things to me that it's going to help get me into bed with you, because it won't!"

"Then I'll have to try another tack. How about if I say nasty things to you?" Amusement welled up in his eyes.

She looked down at him, a dark satyr, his eyes heavy with languorous warmth, a mischievous smile playing on his lips. A woman would have to be certifiably insane to remain immune to this man, she consoled herself, as she smiled back in answer.

"Well? You haven't given me an answer, Nicole. Would it work?"

The images that flashed through Nickie's mind made her blush and she forced herself to look away from his dark gaze. "Why don't we have dessert," she said smoothly, "and I'll think it over."

With a sigh of resignation he sat and reached for a jar that looked like the kind jelly beans come in except that it was full of perfect red raspberries. Chef Boret had given them a pint of heavy cream to go with it. Craig searched vainly for bowls.

"It's unusual for him to forget anything. He must be in love," Craig pronounced with a comical leer. "We'll just have to do without." He poured the cream into the jar of berries, handed Nickie a spoon, and ordered her to dig in.

Sweet and tart exploded in her mouth at once, honing her taste buds to a point of exquisite delight. Craig wiped

51

the juice that was dripping down his chin with the back of his hand.

"This is so good it's sinful," Nickie exclaimed as she lifted another spoon of the dark red berries and rich cream into her mouth. "You're really spoiling me."

"Being spoiled is a highly undervalued pleasure."

As they finished the last of the dessert, Nickie too, lay back, surfeited with good food, laughter, and sunshine. Craig pulled her up.

In one sweeping motion Craig had pulled her toward him and pinned her against his chest. His large warm hands roved sensuously up her back and across her shoulders to finally cup her face. "Nicole, Nicole . . ." he said and sighed. He stared long and hard into her eyes, and she could tell by the way he eased his hold on her, by the softening in his expression, that he instinctively sensed her sudden tension. With her breasts pressed flat against his broad muscular chest and the warm sun on her back, she felt light-headed, intoxicated, really. She closed her eyes and took a deep breath, inhaling the perfume of wild flowers, fresh grass, and the warm, thrilling male scent of the man who held her captive so easily in his arms.

When she opened her eyes again he was smiling at her mischievously, his lips a breathstop away from her own. "You seem to have a drop of berry juice . . . right there," he said, playfully flicking the corner of her mouth with the tip of his tongue. "And over here," he murmured, before running his warm wet tongue across the full curve of her lowe lip. "And if you'll just bear with me another mo- . . ." Then he delicately traced the outline of her with the very tip of his tongue, back and forth ing, maddening pressure.

held her face firmly between his hands, in all

truth Nickie had no urge to pull away. She was mesmerized by his voice, by the tantalizing sensation of his tongue gliding so warmly over her lips; it was a gesture that was not quite a kiss, but far more intimate and arousing than any kiss she could recall having received for a long time.

And then it was over. She opened her eyes, sensing that her tingling lips remained half parted in response to his touch, like some blossoming flower unfolding beneath the warm power of the sun. His broad thumbs feathered lightly across her flushed cheeks. "I could happily finish the task completely," he said in a husky tone, "but something tells me that a splash of cold water might be a better idea right now."

Then he was on his feet, while Nickie took a moment to straighten her top and regain her equilibrium. "Come on," he said lightly. Offering her his hand, he helped her to her feet.

Hand in hand they ran down to the swiftly running water, stooped on the pebbled bank, and splashed icy water on their faces. Nickie, with cheeks aglow and eyes sparkling, watched Craig. There was something so strong about him, something so dominant. She knew that he was a man a woman could lean on. A pity, she remarked to herself, that she wasn't the leaning type.

He turned around. "I thought I felt your eyes boring into my back."

"I was thinking . . . just looking out into space."

"I see." He studied her. "I think you're attracted to me."

"Attracted?" Taken aback, Nickie struggled to regain her aplomb. "Perhaps. If so, it's a purely physical phenomenon. Every animal, from aardvarks to zebras, experi-

53

ences it. It means nothing," she continued lightly, "except that you're an appealing physical specimen."

"Nothing, eh?" With hands cool from the creek, he pushed her down on the yielding ground. Before she could react, his mouth was, once more, on hers. But this time with none of the delicate, deliberately teasing lightness. Her lips, which had been cold, felt as though they were burning, and her back, arching even as she pushed him with her fists, made her body conform to his. His hands moved proprietorially over her body, her shoulders, her neck, her sides, and under the loose material of her sweat shirt, to cup her breasts, which strained against the lacy material of her bra. The moan which started from deep inside her ended with a plea for him to let her go. He answered by pulling up her bra and stretching his hand from one nipple to the other in a gesture that made her shiver from both the pleasure of his touch and the sweet taste of abandon. Yet she misread disdain in his gesture as well, and that made her angry.

"Let me go!" she cried.

His hand caressed the muscle of her calf, moving up to her thigh, to her hip. She didn't even realize that she had shifted weight slightly, allowing him easier access to her hidden places.

"So sweet," he breathed into her ear. "Don't stop me now." He started to unbutton his shirt. Her eyes fastened on the bronze expanse of his chest covered with a tangle of black hairs, and though a part of her she thought was ice had burst into flame in a matter of seconds, she knew what she had to do. She pushed him from her with all her strength and managed to get to her feet. It surprised her that her legs felt wobbly.

"It's been a perfect afternoon. Why spoil it with a less than perfect ending?" There was a tremor to her voice.

"I doubt if we define perfect ending in the same way," he answered with no hint of agitation.

"I think we do."

"Tell you what," she said in a flip voice. "I'll give you your perfect ending once you pitch a perfect game!" She smiled at her cleverness.

"You're on, lady."

"When was the last time someone pitched a perfect game anyway?" she said, and laughed.

"Jergens pitched a no-hitter two years ago, but he gave up two walks. I think Campbell, four years ago."

"That's safe enough! We'd better get going. I have a fight to cover this evening. Peters versus Robinson." She was anxious to get back to familiar territory after this unsettling episode.

"Sounds exciting." Craig cooperated.

"Not really. Boxing is the one sport I loathe. And anyway, Peter's got marshmallows for brains and Robinson is all muscle, including his head.

"Don't say that on the air," Craig warned, "or you might find yourself out of a job."

"I'm tempted. Boxing is tolerable if it's done with finesse, but these guys . . ." She shook her head.

"I'm not a great boxing fan myself. I like fishing. There's nothing like landing a sailfish that's almost got you overboard half a dozen times. It's almost as good as . . . pitching a perfect game," he teased.

"Do you ski? My thing's cross-country," Nickie quickly countered.

Craig sent her a queer grin that made the tiny hairs on the back of her neck bristle.

"Never tried it."

"Well, then, maybe we can go sometime."

"How about tomorrow?" Craig pressed her.

"Sorry, I'm working."

They threw the remains of the picnic lunch in the basket with the soiled linens and dishes. Craig told her he would drop the basket off at the restaurant after he took her back to her car.

The drive back seemed shorter than the one coming, perhaps because it was filled with idle, pleasant chatter, perhaps because once again Nickie knew where she was going. She could handle her life . . . she hoped.

Back at the park, she thanked Craig for the afternoon and for lunch. He saluted jauntily and admitted that he had seen her play the entire ball game and that she really was terrific. He told her she could play on his team any day.

On her way home, Nickie found that she was smiling. She even sang—something she didn't even do in the shower because "tone deaf" would be too nice a way to describe her singing voice.

CHAPTER FIVE

Nickie did not enjoy covering the fight that evening. Always a brutal sport, this match was not saved by the elegance or grace that many better-known boxers display. She scribbled her notes, and when the final bell sounded, she left, not staying around to catch the pearls of wisdom that might fall unbidden from the fighters' lips. She stopped off at the station to tape the scores and a few slightly disparaging comments about tonight's fighters and bloodthirsty audience. Attempting to end her segment on the upbeat, she implored her audience to support Seattle's team in the first national Rubik's cube championship to be held the following week. Their team, she claimed, showed Seattlites to have both an uncommon dexterity matched by a rare brilliance.

As she left the recording booth, she passed Stan Metz and the sound engineer, who looked at her as if she had gone off the deep end.

"Alexander," Stan Metz barked at her as she was disappearing around the corner.

"Yes?"

"You've got twenty-four hours to shape up, or you'll be seeing the back end of the unemployment line! Rubik's cube competition, my whazizz!"

"Don't be so narrow, Stan. There's a wide world of sports out there." Nickie mouthed the cliché cheerfully. Stan was a dolt and he wore blinders, but not even bad fights or Stan Metz could destroy her vaguely troubled happiness.

It was good to get home. This afternoon she had barely touched base. She just had time to shower and change before she had to be at the fight. Now, although it was almost eleven, she made no move to go to bed. She changed into a comfortable cotton nightgown, made herself a cup of cocoa, and curled up in her favorite chair, the overstuffed chintz Queen Anne that clashed dreadfully with the rest of her modern decor. She got up to put an old Barbra Streisand album on the stereo, turned her chair to face the window, and smiled happily to herself as she gazed at Mount Rainier bathed in moonlight, sipped the steamy chocolate, which made little beads of perspiration form on her nose, and listened to the haunting strains of Streisand's torch songs.

Maybe she had been wrong about baseball players. Maybe they weren't all narrow-minded and macho men. But then again, it didn't matter much. Craig Boone might prove that she had a few misconceptions, but it wouldn't change her life, only her way of thinking. The years in her twenties and early thirties would be dedicated to building a career. Then there would be time for marriage with someone of like mind. She would *never* fall in love with a ballplayer. She was destined for other things—to leave her mark on the world of sports coverage, to show that women's sports were as challenging as men's, and that there was excitement in sports other than just baseball, basketball, and football. Not that, she thought with wry self-deprecation, someone like Craig Boone would fall in love anyway. He came off as an untrustworthy ladies' man, too smooth for her tastes.

Deep in thought, she didn't hear the phone until its third ring. "Hello."

"I've been thinking about you all evening." Craig's voice was resonant.

Nickie tried to control her racing heart.

He went on, "I'm beginning to feel about you the way I do about Mell Crandell." He mentioned the Vikings' catcher. "You give out the right signals, call for the right pitch at the right time."

"Craig, please. Don't say that."

"Why not?"

"Because I have one major flaw," she said softly. "I tend to take people at face value. I don't want to believe your words because I know they probably translate to, 'I want to make love.' "

There was only silence on the line. Nickie drew an erratic, sharp doodle on the scratch pad next to her phone.

"I hate whatever happened to you in your life to make you so bitter and frightened. I hate the guy or guys who ran out on you and that blasted accident that made you an orphan," Craig said finally. "Life doesn't have to be like that. I want to show you that it can be different. Better, Nicole."

Nickie's knuckles were white as she clutched the phone.

"That's sweet . . . but nobody has to take care of me. I'm a big girl and I'm doing all right by myself."

Nickie could hear only a slight static on the line, for Craig was silent.

"It's late. I've got to go now, Craig. Good night and thanks for calling. Really."

She laid the phone gently down on the receiver and

stood there looking at it while the needle of her stereo hissed and slid over the smooth part of the record album long after the final notes had faded away.

Nickie passed the next week in a daze. She did her work automatically, but the enthusiasm that had marked her reports was missing. The Vikings were on the road, playing first San Francisco and then Dallas. Nickie suspected the reason for her discontent and didn't like it.

One day, as she opened the newspaper to the sports page, her eye fastened on a picture of Craig in uniform as he was kissed by the president of his fan club. The camera had captured Craig's sheepish grin and the naked adoration on the girl's face as she stood on her toes to reach his lips. Knowing full well that most baseball players' fan clubs consisted of star-struck twelve-year-old boys, Nickie was more than a little taken aback by the picture in front of her. This fan looked as if she were about nineteen or twenty. Long, light-colored tresses curled fetchingly about a face that was pixyish for its nose, sultry for its mouth, and dazzling, if the newspaper picture bore any resemblance to her, for its general cast. Right below it was a smaller picture of Craig, this time in a dark blue pinstripe suit and red tie. He was accepting an award from the Children's Hospital for his role in raising funds for a new rehabilitation wing. A beaming woman and child stood just off to the side looking too proud, Nickie surmised, to be mere onlookers. For a split second she imagined them as his wife and son but dismissed the thought. Craig was known as one of Seattle's eligible bachelors and not even the great Boone could pull off a secret family! Nonetheless, the pictures were unsettling. Her mouth set in a grim line, Nickie folded the newspaper and dropped it in her wastepaper basket. She couldn't, she reminded herself, say that she was surprised at seeing concrete proof of his various women. It was just that she had let down her defenses a little and that had been a mistake she wouldn't repeat. Men like Craig, as the proverbial sailor, had a woman in every port, and with Craig's looks and panache he probably had two or three. The Vikings would be returning Monday for a home game and from that time on, raspberries and cream notwithstanding, her relationship with him would be strictly business.

In the outer office Ruthanne, who had been typing quickly away on the new I.B.M. Selectric, looked at Nickie with concern as she obligingly rummaged in her desk drawer for the two requested aspirins.

The next Sunday her phone rang more than usual. With steely determination Nickie refused to answer it, though the jangling seemed to echo in her eardrums even when there was quiet.

The day of the first returning home game dawned bright and cool. Groggily rubbing her eyes to the rhythm-and-blues wake-up music of her clock radio, Nickie reached over to shut it off. She pulled her feather quilt, its purple satin worn from years of snuggling, over her. She would sleep awhile longer. For some reason she had awakened during the night, once to get a glass of water, once to check that she had locked the door, and then again to open her bedroom window a crack.

When finally she rolled out of bed, she gave herself a leisurely honey and oatmeal facial, dressed, and made up with more than her usual care. It was important to be well-groomed in business, and since lack of sleep always left circles under her eyes, she really ought to compensate for it.

With hair pinned up in a knot and long tendrils framing her face, with her raw silk blouson jacket in deep burgundy, which she had splurged shamelessly to purchase, Nickie surveyed her reflection with some satisfaction. The looks to which she had always been indifferent were oddly becoming a source of pride to her.

After a late breakfast of orange juice and toast, Nickie headed for the station. She wanted to pick up her tape recorder and some notes which she had assembled on the opposing team.

Stan Metz was there to greet her, which he did with a slow and meaningful glance at the wall clock in Ruthanne's office. "Eleven o'clock is too early to come in. I wouldn't want you to exhaust yourself."

The sarcasm was not lost upon Nickie, who answered sharply. "The job gets done, Stan. That's all that should concern you. If you want someone to punch a clock, you've got the wrong person."

"You're not telling me anything I don't know." Metz turned on his heel, and with a face mottled from rage, he stomped out leaving the two women in the outer office.

Ruthanne raised her eyebrows and grimaced at her boss's back. "He can't do a thing about it, because, honey, this station has never had higher ratings than since you've come. I would be the last to lie and tell you the mail and calls have been all positive, because you know they haven't, but at least we got them listening."

"It's a classic case of impotent rage," Nickie said with a defiant toss of her head. "I really don't know what he's got against me. But whatever it is it's his problem."

"The only thing he's got against you is your gender and your success. It goes against everything he's been taught to believe. Forget it."

"I will. I've got to cover the Vikings game this afternoon anyhow, and I certainly don't want my mind muddled up with thoughts of Stan Metz and male chauvinism."

Nickie left the station as soon as possible to arrive early at King Dome Stadium. Sitting in the press box, she imagined herself out there on the pitcher's mound, the game that would win or lose the Series. She knew it was a fantasy that women weren't supposed to have, but she had never been one to bow to convention.

The stands began to fill up with spectators and the press box with reporters. Almost as much as she enjoyed the game itself, Nickie got pleasure from the ball park ambiance. The vendors hawking their popcorn and soft drinks, the subdued excitement of the crowd, gave her a feeling of well-being. It was comfortable knowing that some things never change.

The feeling disappeared the moment she became aware that the Vikings were in their dugout and was replaced by an inability to sit still. Knowing full well that she couldn't report on the game while pacing around the stadium, she forced herself to calm down and pay attention to the action that was about to start.

The opposing team was up at bat first. Craig Boone was the starting pitcher. As he stood on the mound winding up, his eyes scanned the press box. Nickie knew he was seeking her, yet she refused to meet his gaze. The moment passed. When next she looked up his brow was furrowed in concentration, and she knew that his mind was devoid of any thought save how to best strike out the hitter. Surprisingly, the tone was immediately set for this game. After two balls and one strike, the batter doubled to left field. The second man singled, and after the third batter struck out, the next one hit a booming triple to the center field wall. So it went. Craig's timing was off, and no amount of hitting by his teammates could save the day. The game was lost by an ignominious score of eight to three.

Her mouth agape, Nickie didn't bother to close it, so stunned was she by the whiplashing to which the Vikings had just been subjected. By the bottom of the eighth the stands were half empty as fans left in disgust. Her pad was full of notes on errors and bad plays of which not a few had been Craig's direct responsibility. Great heroes die young, she thought ruefully.

As Nickie went on the air that night, she knew that she should not be suffering guilt pangs for what she was about to broadcast. This was her job, and personal feelings had nothing to do with business. People didn't get ahead by being soft. Wars were not won with pity, and the world of sports reporting was a bloody battlefield with more than one past reporter selling shoes today.

But still, as she detailed the game, leaving little out and sparing no feelings with her acerbically witty commentary, she knew that neither Craig nor any other Viking would ever again think of her as a friend. Those were the breaks, she rationalized. She would just have to hope that Craig and Company would be mature about it. Ballplayers come and go, but jobs like hers were a rare plum.

Stan Metz greeted her with the first sincere smile she had ever seen on him. "Not bad. Maybe there's hope for you yet."

"Thanks," Nickie muttered.

She turned up the collar of her trench coat, stuck her hands in her pockets, and left without even saying good-bye to Ruthanne, who watched her interestedly as she pretended to file papers. She didn't mean to slight Ruth-anne and Ruthanne knew it. Never very good at small talk and gossip, Nickie didn't have many friends. Ruth-anne was one of the few.

Her broadcast had been snappy, and Nickie knew she should be happy. But somehow she wasn't. She walked around the block a few times before getting into her car and heading home.

Hardly had she time to unbelt her coat and close the apartment door before the phone rang. It was, as she had feared, Craig.

"*Et tu, Brutus?*"

"Very melodramatic," Nickie answered acidly. "I didn't know you went in for that."

To her surprise, Craig laughed uproariously. Since she didn't see anything particularly amusing, she stood there, the receiver cradled between shoulder and ear, feeling rather put off.

"I understand ambition," he said. "I didn't know how right I was when I remarked that you were not a simper-ing type. It seems I don't have a friend in the media. Not that I need one, of course." His tone was teasing.

Slowly an idea which she didn't like took form in Nick-ie's mind. Awash in indignation, she blurted out her an-ger, "So that's why the sweet words and sweetmeats you plied me with. You wanted to buy my cooperation. Have you found suddenly that your arm is going? Is that it? And you wanted me to keep your secret safe?"

"You don't really believe that, Nicole."

Nickie picked up the cockiness of his tone.

"Sure, I played a lousy game today. It happens to the best of us. Mickey Mantle had his bad days too. That's all there is to it. Nobody's perfect. Even *your* broadcasts

65

occasionally leave something to be desired. What are you doing tomorrow?" Off balance at the abrupt change of topic, Nickie didn't have time to lie.

"I'm going cross-country skiing."

"Good. I'm coming along."

Nickie was not sure she had heard right.

"I hadn't heard myself invite you. I was intending to go alone."

"You issued a vague invitation. Don't you remember? All I'm doing is collecting on a promise."

"Promises, promises," she answered fliply. "And you said you'd pitch a perfect game."

"The season's not over yet." His voice had a steely edge to it. "I do believe you'll come through on your second promise as well."

"I don't know what you're talking about," Nickie said and gulped audibly.

"Yes, you do. Now what time should I pick you up?"

"I want to go skiing tomorrow, Craig. I don't want to be held up by a novice."

"Be ready at six sharp."

The phone clicked in her ear before Nickie had time to utter the "okay" that was on her lips.

CHAPTER SIX

Nickie looked at the clock. It was a quarter of six. Surveying herself in the mirror, she grimaced slightly. In her red knickers that were one size too large (she had lost weight since starting this job), her navy cotton turtleneck that was nubby from countless washings, and her bulky white mohair, she was anything but a fashion plate. Of course the object of her attire was comfort, and she had never before given a thought to its appearance. Clothed in three layers, for she also wore a net undershirt, the only indication anybody could get that she was a nubile young woman was in her choice of color.

An aficionada of cross-country skiing, she knew that the skier is like a furnace, producing enormous quantities of energy. It was important to be able to peel or add layers of clothing according to the amount of body heat produced. Even in the summer the variations of outside temperature could be significant high up in Mount Rainier where they would be headed.

She hurried to the refrigerator in order to pack her rucksack with chicken salad sandwiches she had made last night. She poured hot coffee into a thermos and on impulse added a touch of brandy from the nearly full bottle that had stayed in the back of her cupboard since last

Christmas. She wanted to be downstairs before Craig came.

She was too late. Just as she gathered up her birch and hickory skis, her bamboo poles, and her waxing kit, there was a rap at the door. Opening it, she took a step out at the same time Craig took a step in. There was a knock as metal skis hit wooden ones.

"Too bad. If our skis hadn't tangled, we would have," Craig said in greeting.

"Hi. I'm ready to go. Just let me get my key." Nickie was talking fast.

"Don't I get the grand tour?" Standing just inside the door, Craig looked around with evident interest. "Nice view," he observed. I like your stained glass." He pointed to the plaques with which Nickie had decorated her windows. "Did you make them?"

"Yes. Back in the days when I had time on my hands. They're pretty amateurish."

"On the contrary. They're interesting. Just like the artist." Craig, she noticed, was a picture of sartorial elegance in kid leather boots, blue knickers that looked as soft as cashmere, and a blue nylon anorak on top. He was carrying shiny aluminum skis and poles, the new waxless type that cost a fortune. Most men would have looked overdressed in such an outfit, but Craig, with his rugged, untamed air, could sell a million of those outfits were Madison Avenue to grab him. Nickie smiled thinking that he looked much more put together than she. Setting her sights on the day ahead, she followed Craig out the door.

As fast as he drove, the ride up Mount Rainier just below the tree line was still close to two hours. In the winter Nickie found plenty of trails close to home, but at this time of year that was not possible.

68

The ski area, when they finally arrived, was completely deserted. That was not surprising, since it had been forty-five minutes since they had passed another vehicle on the road. It was much too early for the downhill skiers, and most cross-country buffs were still enjoying toasted marshmallows and country club pools to even consider such a drive for a pleasure that in a few months would be available in their own backyards.

"I warned you, didn't I, that this would be a long ride?"

"So you did. I'm not objecting." Cramped from sitting so long in the car, Craig stretched his six-foot-one-inch frame. "Well, Teach, teach me. I think you'll find I'm an A student."

"As soon as I wax my skis. Here, will you hold these steady?" She leaned her skis against him while starting the burner she carried to melt the wax. "There are different waxes for different ski conditions," she explained as she worked. "I'm using an all-purpose one now, since I expect the run will be fairly easy." The flame on her torch ignited, and she worked rapidly to melt and smooth the wax onto the skis, always making sure to keep the torch moving so as not to scorch the bottom of her skis.

"There. That ought to do it," she said with satisfaction at the competent way she had handled the whole process. Craig might be a great athlete and shrewd businessman, but this was her turf and there could be no doubt that she knew what she was doing.

"Okay. Now for the lesson and for one little warning. If you hold me up too much, I'll go on without you. So pay attention."

"Yes, sir," Craig joshed.

Nickie glowered at him. "If you can walk, you can ski cross-country. It's really very simple and almost impossi-

69

ble to hurt yourself. Injuries simply don't happen in cross-country. Now watch me and try to do exactly what I do."

She showed him the basic body position with knees slightly bent, upper body tilted forward, and head up. She demonstrated the walk, the glide, the step turn, and the kick turn. She found a small incline and made sure he understood the various uphill techniques: the herringbone, the side step, and straight uphill climbing. Though she had expected, indeed hoped, that he would be a bit clumsy, he proved able to master the techniques almost immediately.

She shot him a disturbed look that he interpreted correctly.

"I'm a runner," he told her by way of explanation. "Every morning before breakfast I do eight miles in season or out. It's the best training."

"Well, then, I'm sure you'll have no trouble today. You'll probably outdistance me," she said with a hint of mournfulness. "The mark of the best cross-country skier is tremendous stamina and the ability to go ten or twenty miles at a speed that would destroy most people. But then again," she brightened visibly, "you may not. You have the stamina, but you don't have the skill."

"Give me five minutes," he replied cockily.

Nickie didn't answer. Beckoning him to follow with a curve of her head, she pushed off on her poles. She knew that her technique, as she pushed hard with her skis so that she would spring from one ski to the other in a gliding motion, was flawless.

The park, in the rarified atmosphere of the mountain, was crisscrossed with hiking trails. Rather than skirting the pine forest, Nickie chose a trail which plunged directly into it. Immediately submerged in a dark green cocoon, she emptied her mind of all thought. Where before all had been merely quiet, now the silence had a muffled quality to it. The huffing of their breath and the gliding of their skis on the soft-packed powdery snow were the only sounds. Even the occasional pine cone which fell landed noiselessly.

Nickie adjusted her cap, for her self-propelled wind was making her ears sting. She breathed deeply of the clean smell of pine needles and smiled to herself. She loved these intimate times in the woods, when no matter what was happening in her life she felt at peace. There was no unharmonious note in this world of white, green, and brown.

She heard the kick-glide of skiing rhythm behind her and knew that he had caught on. He sounded every bit as expert as she.

"Look at that tree," she called out. Unusual for a pine, it was gnarled and bent like a lamp post.

Craig told her to stop while he crouched over some animal tracks which circled the tree in deep indentations, crossed the trail a little farther on, and then disappeared beyond the crowded trees. Nickie gasped and pointed wordlessly at a gray fox that she had just glimpsed running with ears flattened and tail flying out behind it.

They continued on, following offshoot trails deeper and deeper into the forest. At some point, exactly when, Nickie couldn't recall, Craig took the lead. They paused occasionally, once at a crystal-clear brook, only half frozen, which meandered lazily around hummocks and fallen branches, and once on the approach to a yawning crevasse which, with its many-hued layers of rock in odd formation, made Nickie thrill as she imagined the first explorer to chance upon the Grand Canyon had.

A high point came some miles later when they reached

71

the halfway mark of the circular route they had finally decided on. Craig held up his arm for Nickie to stop, and with a finger to his lips, he showed her what he was observing. There, not fifty yards away in the shadow of the trees, stood a velvet brown doe, a benign glaze over her eyes as she suckled her young. The fawns stood on spindly legs at her underbelly. Even from that distance, Nickie saw or perhaps sensed the trust and contentment in the innocent faces. Not wanting to disturb, Nickie tried to control her breathing so that she could blend in with the August quietude. Craig looked at her, then back to the doe. The intelligent concentration in his eyes sent shivers up and down her spine.

Something, perhaps a sixth sense, made the doe look up and straight at them. She stiffened, and as if with the exchange of an ancient signal, the fawns broke away and ran on wobbly legs to disappear with her as through a verdant curtain. The moment was gone, but its magic lingered.

The temperature dropped and their strides became brisker, almost like joggers'. Craig suggested that they stop for lunch, and as soon as she heard his words Nickie became aware of her gnawing hunger pangs. They found a clearing under twin fir trees. Sinking thankfully onto a flat rock, Nickie watched while Craig gathered wood for a fire. She felt warm in spite of the unexpected cold, yet tired. She hadn't expected to go quite this far.

"You must have been a boy scout," she said as he ignited the fire on his first try.

"Actually, I was kicked out of cub scouts for almost setting fire to my tent." He eagerly bit into the proffered chicken salad sandwich. "Curried chicken salad—a repast fit for kings and ex-cub scouts."

Despite herself, Nickie flushed with pleasure.

"I'm glad you like it. Some people consider eating curry cruel and unusual punishment."

"Not me. I could even sprinkle cumin and coriander on apple pie."

She handed him a plastic cup filled with hot coffee laced with brandy.

"I know the cups aren't Limoges, but nobody's perfect."

She smiled ironically, for the obvious dig in her comment and for the hidden association that the word "perfect" had taken on for them.

Craig took a big gulp of the brew. "If you're trying to get me riled, you're not going to succeed. I'm having too fine a time out here with the lady of my choice—Miss Ice Queen."

She ignored the nomenclature and continued, "But there are several *choice* ladies out there, aren't there? I saw a couple of interesting pictures of you in the newspaper."

"Ah-hah!" he chuckled. "Jealousy rears its head!"

"Don't be ridiculous!" she snapped.

Though she could have used a bit more rest, she didn't like the turn the conversation had taken but knew it had been her own fault.

She rose. "We'd better get going. The temperature seems to have dropped. We don't want to let our muscles tighten." Her voice was sharply impersonal.

They threw snow on the fire and stamped out the remaining cinders. Reaching out as far as her arms would permit, she pushed off with her poles. It had gotten colder, she realized, as soon as she glided down the steep incline just beyond their campsite, for her skis no longer felt right. She turned to call out to Craig, who was trailing her.

"I've got to stop to wax these. . . . *Aieee!*" She was thrown in the air and landed with a jarring bump in a tangle of arms and legs. She thought she knew what it would feel like if the end of the world ever came.

"Nicole, Nicole, are you hurt?" Before she had time to know, herself, if she was in one piece, Craig was upon her, his face lined with worry. Winded, she was unable to utter more than a groan. Gingerly, Craig lifted her head looking for lacerations. There were none. Next he examined her arms. Her left leg was fine. When he tried to move her right leg, she let out a bellow of pain.

"Don't touch it!" she cried. "Just leave me alone for a while!" She let her head fall back in the snow. Craig took off his cap and put it under her. Within minutes the wet snow seeped through her knickers and sweaters, causing her teeth to chatter.

"We've got to get you out of here," Craig announced.

"What happened anyway?" Nickie stammered.

"That little hummock you sailed over was a hidden tree stump. It would have fooled anybody."

"That's crazy. Things like this aren't supposed to happen in cross-country skiing. It's the safest sport around."

"I'm going to pull you up," Craig said tersely. "See if you can lean on me."

With one swift motion he had her upright. As soon as her right foot touched the ground, Nickie thought she was going to faint.

"I can't," she gasped. "I think my ankle is broken."

"Nonsense," he said as he examined it gently. "It looks badly bruised, but that's all."

"That's all!" she exclaimed crossly. "My whole body is exploding with pain and you say 'that's all.' Go on without me. Just leave me here to die."

74

Craig laughed. "Things can't be too bad if you still have your sense of humor. Now it seems we're going to have to be intelligent about this."

"We're at least five miles from the car. The only thing you can do is build me a fire and go back for help."

"Leave you here alone? That's absurd! I'm going to carry you back."

"Impossible! They'll find both our bodies here."

"You'll have to leave your skis and poles," Craig said apologetically.

"Never!"

"I'll buy you new ones."

"I don't want new ones. I want those."

"You're acting childish," Craig said with an air of authority. Without another word Nickie found herself hoisted over his shoulder, her head aimed perilously toward the ground.

"You don't have to handle me like a sack of dirty laundry," she complained.

Craig chuckled as he moved swiftly off on skis.

"Let me down! I'm getting dizzy!" She kicked against his chest with one soft leather boot.

"Don't be naughty or I'll spank that bottom. It's in an ideal position for it."

Nickie squeezed her eyes shut and closed her mouth and wondered how she had ever let herself get into such a situation. She also marveled at how he, a first-time skier, managed so well and carried her with such seeming effortlessness. He could have been racing for years for the little time it took to arrive at the car. He deposited her unceremoniously in the backseat. She sneezed.

"You're going home to bed. I'll send my own doctor up to see you."

75

In too much pain to argue, though she would have liked to tell him he could simply drop her off at an emergency room somewhere, she mumbled a curt thanks. What an ignominious ending to the day. It was he, the "bumbling beginner," who was supposed to have the problems, if any were to be had. Why couldn't things turn out the way they were supposed to? Although she hadn't noticed it on the way up, the ride home was long, tiresome, and even in the cushiony comfort of a Maserati, bumpy. Not what could be termed a stoic, Nickie spent the entire trip agonizing silently over her foot.

As Craig pulled up in front of her apartment, Nickie got up on one elbow and realized that she was, once more, going to be carried. This time Craig held her in both arms. It was infinitely more pleasant. As he passed with her through the lobby door, Nickie caught the shocked expression on the face of her gossipy first-floor neighbor and realized with a sinking heart what that woman and the rest of the building would soon be thinking. Although she was independent and proud of it, Nickie didn't like the idea of rumors, especially false ones, circulating about her. She handed Craig her key, which she had had the foresight to fish from her zippered rucksack while she was still in the car. Still holding her, he managed to unlock the door and to kick it open.

"You can put me on the sofa."

"Which way is the bedroom?" Without waiting for an answer, he headed for the slightly ajar door flanked by two dragon trees. He laid her down gently on the bed. Nickie was glad she had put on the bedspread, unlike some mornings when she was too rushed to take the time. He put a hand on her forehead.

"Whatever else you've got, you're also coming down with a cold."

"Nonsense." She sneezed.

"We'll let the doctor decide if it's nonsense or not," Craig said firmly. "I'm going to get you some aspirin and an ice pack for that ankle. Then you're going to rest until he comes. Understood?" There was a gruff tenderness in his voice and Nicole couldn't help but be touched. It had been such a long time since anyone had dared to take her in hand like this.

"Yes, Nurse Boone," Nickie teased, but still with some measure of gratefulness in her voice. Her whole leg was beginning to throb, she had chills, and her head was pounding. Fatigue was making it increasingly difficult for her to keep up the banter. She thought that maybe Craig was right, and she was coming down with something. Whatever it was, it had better not last long. She couldn't afford to miss covering any home games.

Her eyes half closed, she was only dimly aware of it when Craig pressed his lips to her forehead and slipped out the door to let her sleep.

CHAPTER SEVEN

Dr. Wiley turned out to be a curt, no-nonsense doctor of the school that believed physicians to be just a notch below God. Though she found his manner irksome, especially when he refused to answer her questions about the new field of sports medicine or even to acknowledge that he had heard of them, Nickie was relieved at his diagnosis of a torn ligament and a virus. His cure called for bed rest, and as she had predicted, an Ace bandage.

Before leaving, Craig had explained that he wouldn't be seeing her for a few days because of the team's heavy practice schedule. "Then we're on the road again. You'll be watching the Chicago game on TV, won't you?" he had asked her then.

"I wouldn't miss it," Nicole had promised him. He smiled, she remembered, and after apologizing again for having to leave her on her own, he promised to send his Chinese manservant over to take care of her.

Nicole had thought he was joking at the time. Who in the world actually had a manservant? It sounded too much like a PG-rated movie to be for real.

Sure enough, Jo-Jo turned up on her doorstep that evening, turning out to be—she had to smile—cheerful and of impeccable manners and enviable culinary skill.

"The Chinese," he told her when she complimented him on his chicken soup and rice and told him it hit the spot precisely, "are a people of infinite wisdom."

She believed him.

The next day, when she wasn't sleeping she was eating. With Jo-Jo's poached salmon, welsh rarebit, and gallons of camomile tea, she had never had such a gourmet bland diet. She asked him how he liked working for Craig. He turned out to be Craig's biggest fan.

"That Mr. Boone, he's the best," Jo-Jo said proudly. Nickie gave him a noncommittal smile.

A masseuse showed up the following morning; compliments of Craig Boone, of course. It was Nickie's first massage ever, and she thoroughly enjoyed the pummeling and pressing. With all the pampering she had enjoyed the last day and a half, she was loath to admit that, even though she hobbled a bit, she felt too well to justify another day at home.

On the day of the Chicago game she called Stan Metz to tell him that she would be in later on to report the score. He offered to let her use a special telephone hookup from her own phone. Since there was nothing going on in live sports that day in Seattle, there was no reason why she could not report on the Vikings game that evening from the comfort of her bedside after viewing it from her own twenty-one-inch R.C.A.

"Thanks, Stan. That's awfully kind of you." *Uncharacteristically kind,* she thought.

"Harumph. Well, be sure to inhale steam before you go on. I don't want you sounding nasal."

"Sure, Stan. Will do."

Slightly uncomfortable about the arrangement, Nickie decided there was no sense in dwelling upon it and dismissed it from her thoughts in order to open her door to an urgent ring. A strapping young man in a messenger's uniform stood dwarfed behind an enormous bouquet of at least a gross of wild flowers. She gasped, flabbergasted, before the magnificent array that had been prepared with studied abandon by some meticulous florist. Regaining her aplomb just in time to rummage in her purse for a bill with which to tip him, Nickie realized, even as she gushed her thanks, that she was going on as if this messenger had personally scoured remote tropical mountaintops in search of these perfect buds.

After closing the door behind the grateful messenger, for she hadn't looked too closely at the denomination of the bill which she had handed him, she rummaged carefully in the bouquet on her kitchen table for a note. There, hidden among the purple flowers in the center, she found it.

Nicole, think of me tonight. I'll be playing this game for you.

It was unsigned, but a signature, of course, would have been superfluous. Nickie sighed. Whatever he lacked, Craig more than made up for with style.

Amusement flickered in her eyes when Jo-Jo arrived a few hours later. Her apartment was beginning to remind her of Grand Central Station. When she was well she rarely had visitors. He brought her dinner with him, a fettucini in cream sauce and veal *piccante,* which was delicately flavored with lemon and butter.

"It's a good thing I'm going to work tomorrow. A few more days of this, and I'd have to join Weight Watchers!" she groused indulgently.

"You could use the pounds." Jo-Jo shook his head. Where before she had looked fragile, hard work and hurried meals now lent her prominent cheekbones a gaunt look. That is, when she neglected to use rouge.

"Are you staying around to watch the game?" Nickie asked.

"Not tonight. The boss will be home tomorrow, and he'll be wanting the place shipshape. You take care and call if you need anything."

Nickie wondered if Jo-Jo took care of Craig as well as he was taking care of her. She hobbled into bed after Jo-Jo left. Though she was surrounded by magazines and half-read books, she was unable to concentrate on the written word. She was, in fact, unable to concentrate on anything except the upcoming game, wild flowers, and Stan Metz's unusual offer of the home hookup. He was not known, in the trade, for his generosity of spirit.

Her fettucini and veal got cold as she mulled over the past days. What did it all mean? Craig Boone was doing his charming best to seduce her. He was, she was convinced, the playboy type, and she, though pretty, beautiful even, was not the seductive type who attracted hordes of men, least of all playboys. Stan Metz was suddenly nice. She was stuck in bed when she wanted to be out working. Everything was topsy-turvy.

She switched on her television set and checked with the radio station to make sure there would be no hitch with the phones. All was well. The game would be starting in a matter of minutes. How she wished she could be out there in Chicago's Comiskey Park covering the game for a national network! She would be the first woman ever to do so and the one to break down the final barriers of male dominance in the field of broadcasting. That was her dream and her ambition, and—she drew her lips into a tight line—she would get there some day!

Craig was the starting pitcher. The stadium was filled with Chicago fans. It looked like a sellout crowd. Nickie could practically smell the hotdogs and feel the electrically charged excitement of thousands as Craig got ready to throw his first pitch. Chicago had a good team this year and odds were that Seattle would lose this one, especially because of a couple of key injuries.

Before the fans knew what had happened, Craig had struck out the first three hitters. No one had even touched the ball. With the Vikings up, there was only slightly more action. One player singled, but the rest were pop-ups or easy fly balls. The second inning was more of the same with Craig striking out the leadoff hitter and getting the next two hitters to ground out. If things kept up this way, Nickie mused, this game might not last through two commercials. The camera panned a close-up of Craig and the steely set of his jaw made her shudder. She was glad he was not pitching to her! Three more innings passed and neither team had any runs. The only problem—Nickie blanched at the thought—was that Craig had given up no hits or walks and the Vikings had made no errors. It was the bottom of the sixth, and Craig was thus far pitching the proverbial perfect game! He couldn't keep this up, Nickie consoled herself. A perfect game only occurred once every few years. Nonetheless, fear gripped her. Why, oh why had she ever made that silly promise about getting his perfect ending if he pitched a perfect game? When would she learn to think before she spoke? Well, no matter. He must know she had said it in jest.

In the top of the sixth, the Vikings had a man on second and a man on first. Craig was up at bat. He hit a solid line drive, bringing two men home and leaving him with a double. The score was now two to nothing in favor of the

Vikings. The next man struck out and it was Chicago at bat.

Craig was still pitching, with Seattle's relief pitchers twiddling their thumbs in the dugout. Perhaps, with the first six innings as they were, Chicago didn't have a chance to recoup. Craig's psychological advantage over them was too great. Like a gambler with a winning streak, Craig pitched smoothly and artfully. His arm was well oiled and he moved to a rhythm no one else heard. An uneasy pall had fallen over the stadium back in the third inning, and with Chicago's diehard fans, the atmosphere, even on television, came across as distinctly funereal. There was a time, in the ninth inning, when Nickie prayed traitorously along with the Chicago fans that Craig would muff it. With three balls and no strikes, he almost walked the third hitter. Unfortunately, he followed them with two good strikes and then the hitter flied out. The game was over.

His teammates went wild, jumping all over him and lifting him to their shoulders in a triumphal march. When finally they put him down, he was almost hidden from view with all the media people who surrounded him, eager to record his first words. ABC held out its microphone in front of him.

"How does it feel, Mr. Boone, to have pitched Seattle's first perfect game?"

Craig winked broadly into the camera.

"There's only a few things in this world that feel better."

Nickie thought she would die! She slid down into her bed and pulled the covers over her head. It was not going to be easy doing the evening sports news update. Seattle would expect her to gush over Craig Boone and report the game in exuberant detail! She wasn't sure she could rise to the occasion.

Of course, being a professional, she did as she had to. She suspected that only the people who knew her best could notice the lack of enthusiasm in her voice. That could be explained, if ever brought up, by the defects of technology, what with the double hindrance of telephone and radio. How could she, after all, be anything but happy with Seattle's sterling triumph?

The hours ticked by with Nickie sitting in her living room, her foot raised on a small table. The Vikings were due to fly home tomorrow. That gave her one evening to plan strategy, for she surely wasn't going to sleep with anybody on a dare! The easiest thing would be never to speak to Craig again. That would avoid an ugly confrontation. It wouldn't prove very practical, however, in terms of her career.

After puzzling over various options, she decided that she would simply play dumb, forget that she had made so crazy an offer. This wasn't the Middle Ages, where a person's word sealed their fate. With that question settled, she got up to go to bed.

There was a knock at the door and then a key turned in the lock. Jo-Jo was too much, she thought.

"Are you here to fix me milk and honey?" she called out laughingly. "You're the mother I never had!"

"If it's hot milk and honey you want, I'll be happy to oblige," Craig answered in a booming voice.

She spun around in her chair. A shock wave of pain sliced through her foot.

"What are you doing here? And how dare you come in like that!"

"Thanks for the kudos," Craig replied as he cast a

sweeping glance over her. Nickie became uncomfortably aware that she had nothing on under the Indian print caftan which she often wore when lounging around her apartment.

"Here's your key." He laid it on top of a pile of well-thumbed copies of *Sports Illustrated* in the middle shelf of her étagère.

"You were supposed to return tomorrow," she reiterated in an accusatory tone.

"The team decided to celebrate at home. It was a short game, as I'm sure you know, and with the time difference of two hours, we figured we'd get here when it was relatively early. It's only ten thirty."

That she was behaving rudely penetrated the jumble of thoughts in her mind.

"The game was well played." She knew the compliment sounded grudging, but there were extenuating circumstances. "And, oh! Thanks for the flowers. They're lovely."

Craig stood leaning against the wall next to the door, his arms folded across his chest.

"Are you ready to talk business?" he asked.

"What? Business? I don't know what you're talking about!" she reponded, flustered. Her hands picked up a geode paperweight and put it down. She idly pushed a lamp first to one corner of an end table and then back to the center. She twisted a strand of her long dark hair.

Craig bit his lip as if to keep from laughing. "I thought I'd give you an exclusive interview with reprint rights."

"An interview! That would be sensational. Thanks! Why don't we meet in my office tomorrow afternoon?" she said briskly. *Just keep this impersonal, dear Lord,* she prayed.

"Mind if I have a seat?"

"A seat?" She was beginning to feel like an echo. "I was just getting ready for sleep."

"Surely you can spare the conquering hero a few min-utes of your time?" His smile was vaguely alarming. "I was looking forward to a little . . . *warmer* reception, even from Miss Ice Queen."

Abashed, Nickie touched cold fingers to her temples. "Please do sit down and"—she couldn't resist the dig—"hail, hail!" She went into the kitchen to search for the bottle of champagne which she had gotten as a house-warming present when she first moved into this apart-ment. She was sure it hadn't been drunk, but as she moved pots and pans and empty jars which she had saved for no logical reason, she was unable to find it. She came up, at long last, holding a bottle of ginger ale and two long-stemmed goblets.

"I know Canada Dry isn't Dom Perignon," she lament-ed, "but organization isn't one of my strong points. I can't find the bubbly. It'll show up next time I need a mixer for bourbon."

"That's fine. Your eyes provide all the intoxication I need." Nickie poured the soda, held her glass up, and toasted recklessly.

"Here's to perfect games." As soon as the words were out, she could have bitten her tongue.

"And to perfect endings," Craig rejoined.

"Now wait a minute. I was afraid you'd bring that up. You can't really expect me to . . ."

"Relax. I don't want anything that's not freely given. I thought I made that clear." His gaze was unflinching. "I hope you don't seriously think I played that game tonight

86

just so I could get you to bed? You're lovely to look at, Nicole, but Helen of Troy you're not!"

Nickie turned away. "You don't have to be insulting about it."

"I didn't mean to be."

Nickie picked imaginary lint off the sofa.

Craig continued matter-of-factly, "How are you feeling? Dr. Wiley phoned me in Chicago to tell me about the ligament."

"That was rather presumptuous of him. Whatever happened to confidentiality between physician and patient?"

"He figured I had a proprietary interest. You didn't answer my question."

"Oh, I'm all right." Her manner was casual. Actually, as soon as she put pressure on her foot the pain was excruciating. But as much as she disliked pain she disliked complainers and would not be one. Craig saw through her.

"You don't have to be proud with me."

He moved closer and caught her hand. She returned the slight pressure. As he bent to kiss her, she averted her face. With one hand he tilted her chin up. His thumb stroked one corner of her lips and the sensuality, the dominance so inherent in this seemingly small gesture, made her breath catch in her throat. As he held her chin, she caught the tenderness in his eyes and closed her own. When his lips touched hers she imagined that she felt the kind of shock you get when you shuffle through a thickly carpeted room on a dry winter's day. She felt a freedom and an urge to flee and she knew she was answering his kisses fully.

One part of her said "run!" The other felt powerless to withstand the languorous sensuality which filled her as his mouth worshiped her. It was a feeling she had for so long, and had never, ever felt at this

His lips moved from her mouth to her nape. Bending her head, she obliged him with greater access. His hands and mouth caressed her shoulders and her arms. As his warm lips glided along her arms, she felt that no man in giving so little had ever teased a woman to greater heights of anticipation. His hands stopped at the zippered back of her caftan and Nickie waited with bowed head as with one gentle, yet deft motion he pulled the zipper down. The quiet uncleaving of the metal teeth sounded in her ears with ponderous meaning. His hands spread the loose fabric of her garment to better trace the length of her spine. She shivered and shifted position so that she could look at him. As she did so one loose sleeve of her caftan fell from her shoulder, exposing the slight swell of the upper part of her breast. He pulled the material down, covering her breasts with his palms. His fingers stroked and teased the nipples, which stiffened under his touch. A low sound escaped from the back of her throat as she felt his warm breath on her bosom. He kissed her as she had never been kissed in ways that tortured with delight. Her eyes were half closed when he stopped, but she could feel rather than see his eyes as they studied her, boring into her, discovering her secrets.

When finally he stripped the garment from her, letting it drop to the ground, she knew she was conquered. For a long time he just stared, visually drinking in the vision of her. As he continued to gaze boldly on her naked body, she felt that he possessed her utterly and completely.

Standing before her, he slowly began to unbutton his shirt. As she stared at him, the broad, nut-brown expanse of chest, the total male perfection of his athletic body, shook her. Half naked, he knelt at her side to kiss her hand. Nickie could hardly speak, yet she knew she didn't want him to stop. There burned deep inside her a fire which only he could extinguish.

She reached out to touch him. "You're beautiful," she murmured. She moved her hands slowly over his shoulders and back, loving the smooth, stone-hard feel of him. She breathed deeply of the musky male smell of him. Passing her lips lightly over the muscled column that was his neck she teased his senses with light butterfly kisses. She nuzzled her cheek against the rough hairs that curled like a fan over his chest and felt that there was no place on earth she would rather be.

Lifting her easily, he carried her into the bedroom and onto the bed. She waited as he stepped out of his pants and in that moment realized that she loved this man. The knowledge rocked her, and when he joined her she clung to him with a need that matched his own. She relaxed, letting all tension flow out of her to be replaced by a consuming passion and a desire to please with her touch, her femininity, her love.

"Easy, my love. I've waited too long for this. No need to rush." He kissed her to stifle a reply lest one was forthcoming.

She wrapped her arms around him and covered his face with kisses, his nose, his eyelids, his brow.

"You're so beautiful, so fresh, so vulnerable," he rasped thickly. Starting at her toes, he slowly kissed his way up her body, up her thighs, her hips, her stomach, up, up to her neck and ears and eyes. Slow, mesmerizing kisses. She noticed gratefully that he carefully avoided her bad foot. As she looked down at him, she was struck by the vivid contrast of his jet-black hair with the slight golden down of her arms and thighs, which still glistened from his kisses. She uttered a sound, deeply female in nature, that fell somewhere between a sigh, a moan, and an urging. He was unable to restrain himself any longer.

Nickie tensed with the first sharp pain but relaxed as it melted into a voluptuous sweetness. As she felt her breasts flatten against his chest and her hips and thighs against his, her body conformed naturally to him. They moved together as one. She seemed to envelop him as the dividing line between them evaporated in the heat of their lovemaking. Everything swirled by in misty, blissful undulations. All the feelings which had wrenched her heart these past weeks—desire, denial, fear—were consumed in the full-blown intensity of love fulfilled.

Finally drained, yet curiously complete, they lay side by side on the damp bedsheets, not looking at one another. Nickie knew they had connected in the most elemental of ways. Then an alarming thought entered her head.

"Craig, you don't think"—she hesitated—"that tonight was payment for that deal we talked about, the perfect game business?"

"Of course not, silly. Tonight was sublime . . . perfect even," he teased.

Craig let his hand rest on the barely noticeable roundness of her belly. She nestled against his cheek and with a contented half-smile on her face, she drifted into peaceful sleep.

It was near dawn when Craig awoke. He smiled possessively at the naked sleeping form next to him. Nickie opened her eyes under his scrutiny.

"Do you think I'm a shameless hussy?" she asked sleepily.

"The very worst!" he assured her as he laughingly draped the blanket over her and with one hand curled over her breast returned to sleep.

CHAPTER EIGHT

Despite the next morning's wet weather they decided on a stroll along the waterfront. Gusts of wind and rain blew Nickie's hair back from her face and stung her eyes. Craig, wearing a black oilskin cape which he had picked up at his apartment on the way, looked at her appreciatively. In a yellow slicker which contrasted with her raven-colored hair, Nickie was fetching.

"Are we the only two nuts out walking today?" she asked lightly.

"Probably, but where would the world be if lovers stopped walking in the rain? Do you feel all right on that leg though?"

"Of course. It was nothing major. Let's talk about something more interesting—like the weather."

"Okay." He took her seriously. "Do you enjoy these dark, dank, cloudy days as much as I do? They have substance, mood. What a bore it would be if every day were sunny and bright like an idiotically smiling face that never frowned."

"I know what you mean. Rain reminds me of when I was a kid and I used to curl up in a windowseat with a forever shedding angora cat and piles of old *Reader's Digests.* I would read all the humor sections straight through and watch the rain splatter on the glass. That was before I lost my parents. Afterwards I never found 'Life in These United States' quite so funny.''

Craig looked at her soberly and held out his hand. They walked slowly past the warship *Decatur*, anchored off-shore since 1856, past curio shops, huge warehouses, and past Seattle's most famous gourmet ice cream shop.

"An ice cream cone?" Craig offered.

"A double scoop of French vanilla," Nickie assented.

"I must confess to being an incorrigible ice cream snob," Craig admitted. "I think I would consider going to Philadelphia and back in a day just for a pint of freshly made Bassetts."

"I like the supermarket brands myself," Nickie said, and grinned.

"That figures."

The ice cream shop, spelled shoppe, was decorated in imitation turn-of-the-century art. Factory-made Tiffany lamps and unleaded stained glass, plated wrought iron, and plaster figurines abounded.

"Don't worry. The ice cream's the genuine article," Craig whispered, guessing her thoughts.

The proprietor, his mustachioed face wreathed in smiles, greeted them effusively. Nickie was ashamed of herself for wondering momentarily if it was because they were the only people in the shop.

"It's nice to see two such attractive people out on a day like today," the man boomed. "Vanilla and chocolate?" he repeated questioningly, clearly disappointed at the prosaic choices in flavor. "Let me give you a taste of my amaretto and cream," he offered expansively, "for your sparkling eyes," he directed to Nickie, "and for your good taste," he said to Craig. With that he heaped a third scoop of his newest flavor on top of the cones. He would accept payment for only two scoops.

"So is *he* the genuine article!" Nickie murmured to Craig on their way out.

"What a darling man! But how does he make a living if he insists on giving away his ice cream?" she asked, not even pausing to take a breath between sentences or licks.

"Man does not live by ice cream alone. The world is in love with love," Craig answered.

"I think I am, too, if it means ice cream like this!" Nickie managed between licks.

"I thought you preferred supermarket brands," he countered.

"Oh, let me be with my reverse snobbism!"

Nickie looked up at his smiling eyes. For a fleeting instant she thought that nothing else mattered, that life, after all, was nothing more or less than walking along a pier and eating ice cream cones sprinkled with raindrops.

Where wares were usually peddled on crowded streets, vendors had now moved them out of the rain into jumbled stalls. They stopped at almost every one, admiring hurdy-gurdies, eskimo souvenirs, ceramic honey pots, hand-crafted leather belts, ad infinitum. Nickie had to restrain Craig from buying everything she paused to admire.

"We'll be weighted down like pack mules. I want to enjoy this walk!"

He insisted, however, on buying her a Vikings nightshirt.

"Does this mean you never want me to stop thinking of you, not even when I'm asleep?" she flirted.

"You couldn't stop thinking of me if you tried."

A sharp retort was on the tip of her tongue, which he stifled with a brief, yet warmly persuasive kiss.

93

Ye Olde Curiosity Shoppe, one of Seattle's institutions, beckoned them next with its promise of serendipity. There they browsed among genuine Indian totem poles, magic amulets, and shrunken heads.

"No, Craig, I do not want one of these sitting on my night table," she exclaimed in what she hoped was a light tone as he picked up a wizened specimen by its gray hair. She lost sight of him a minute later as she became caught up in examining antique lace. And actually jumped when a mummy moved from a dark corner to embrace her with ferocious strength.

"How did you do that?"

"I'm a quick-change artist."

"When you're not playing baseball, programming computers, and whatever else you do. Well, you're also a sadist. Remind me never to go to one of those Halloween haunted houses with you." He tried to suppress a smile at her words. With fingers that were sensitive and strong he traced the line of her lips and told her the sound of her voice reminded him of a flute expertly played. Nickie was grateful they were in a public place for she could barely keep her lips from trembling or restrain herself from throwing her arms around the sinewy hardness of his neck.

She felt his eyes devouring her with the same hunger which gnawed so disturbingly at her insides. She stepped back to break the spell. He turned, with a knowing brightness in his eyes, to move toward the front of the store. The unbridled masculinity, the casual elegance with which he moved, reminded her of a snow leopard—wild, untamable, alone on the heights yet sure of its prey. She followed him.

With the dignity that only the supremely self-confident

can muster, he picked up one of those helium balloons that have "I love you" emblazoned across in big letters, tossed a dollar bill on the counter, and with a solemn expression on his face he took her left hand in his and wrapped the string twice around her ring finger.

"There," he said with a satisfied smile. "Now it's official."

"Until I have to take my clothes off."

He smiled wickedly. "I love it when you talk dirty to me."

"You're bizarre," she expostulated in mock exasperation.

No sooner were they outside again than the rain which had changed from a fine mist to a driving downpour caused Nickie to pause in order to pull the strings of her slicker tighter under her chin, thereby loosening her grip on the balloon. It took only seconds for it to fly into the mist.

"Now everybody who sees the balloon will know how I feel about you."

"Or at least the little boy in Spokane who eventually finds it." The rain was streaming down in rivulets along the creases of his cheeks which his smile had forged. It formed droplets on Nickie's eyelashes, blurring her vision. It occurred to neither of them that they might be more comfortable in a warm, dry place. Arm in arm they strolled along the waterfront, not noticing or caring that their feet made squishing sounds in waterlogged shoes or that their pants legs were soaked. They watched a ferry from Juneau unload its Eskimo passengers and its mysteriously crated cargo.

A dockworker ran over to them and excitedly asked

Craig for his autograph. He bellowed for his coworkers to join him. "Yo! Craig Boone here! Boone here!"

He was joined by three strapping young men who insisted on talking with Craig and on getting pointers for their own amateur league. It was to no avail that Craig tried politely to extricate himself from the group, for whenever he made as if to leave they would animatedly recall one of Craig's special victories. They were dyed-in-the-wool fans and that, as Craig later admitted to Nickie, made it exceedingly difficult for him to be rude. It was at the end of the half hour of insistent jocularity that Nickie realized how cold, drenched, and uncomfortable she really was.

"Does this happen to you often?" she asked as they finally broke away.

"All too often. When you're in the public eye everyone considers you fair game. It makes me think at times that I should retire to the North Pole where no one will recognize me. How about it? Will you join me there? I'll build you an igloo with wall-to-wall Congoleum, and we can while away the years rubbing noses."

"Only if you make that genuine oak floors instead of Congoleum," she riposted.

"I'll pitch snowballs and you can broadcast ice fishing competitions. Meanwhile, what do you say we sit down somewhere over a steaming cup of Irish coffee?"

"The way to a woman's heart . . ."

"Is through a mug of Irish coffee," they finished in unison.

They wound up in a cozy little clam house where one Irish coffee became pluralized and the morning stretched into the afternoon. Upon beholding his bedraggled customers their waiter resolutely moved their table in front of a great stone fireplace. He stoked the fire until it roared.

Decorum set aside in the easy atmosphere of the establishment, they removed their shoes and put their feet up to dry.

The splendid glow of the flames, the expertly blended drink, the masculine beauty of Craig, his bones finely molded under the olive skin of his face, the taut muscles of his perfect body making her yearn to reach out and touch him, all worked upon her senses making Nickie feel that she would never stop laughing. She told him seriously how much her career meant to her and of her dreams. He spoke to her of his passion for baseball. He claimed it was a civilized sport, a team sport yet an individual sport, and the only major one in which the man scored rather than the ball. He admitted to her the tight control he had to maintain over himself while pitching. Pitchers are the most visible of all players, for they are involved in every play and are therefore the most psychologically influenced by what happens in the field. He had seen too many pitchers fall apart because of errors made by their teammates. He had never let that happen to him. The set of his mouth was grim as he told her that, and she could sense the mighty powers of concentration which he had to summon to keep that psychological calm while pitching.

They ate steamed clams by the dozen and, in the brief interludes between forkfuls or between the animated pace of their conversation, their eyes would meet, and Nickie would feel her knees begin to shake uncontrollably. When close to five o'clock she glanced at her watch, more out of habit than curiosity, she sat upright, a look of alarm on her face.

"I've got to be at the station! I'm on in less than an hour." She jumped up. Craig settled the bill and dashed out with her. He ran to get his car. Three minutes later it screeched to a halt in front of the curb and barely ten minutes after that she was at the station.

"The news waits for no man," he said laconically.

"Or woman," she said as she ran out of the car. "It was a wonderful day."

"I know," he said a with a touch of melancholy in his voice. "Don't muff the scores now. I'll be tuned in."

"Don't worry. Metz will have them there for me, and I'm in plenty of time to look them over. I'm a quick study!"

Her heart skipped as she watched him drive away, and for the first time since she had started this job, her attention was not wholly devoted to it.

CHAPTER NINE

The next day as Nickie stepped foot inside the station something didn't seem right. Ruthanne didn't come out to greet her and the audio technicians avoided her glance. The piles of sports data from ticker tapes and newspaper and magazine clippings which she had come to expect would be overflowing on her desk were noticeably missing. Facts and figures for today's segment were, however, prominently displayed on her blotter. More ominous than all of that was Stan Metz's mood. The normally dour station manager appeared almost chipper as he stuck his head in the recording booth just before she went on.

Only advance notice that the Black Plague was about to strike could make that man happy, thought Nickie with trepidation. Well, she would worry about that later. Right now she had a report to air. She looked over the notes and scores on her desk. Everything, of course, was on out-of-town games and gotten from wire sources. Nickie had an uncanny ability to look at scores and plays, make sense of them, and fashion them quickly into a coherent and interesting story. Most of all she loved broadcasting baseball news. She respected the sport for the tremendous skill it required at the professional level. She looked forward to broadcasting live games, but of course hadn't the opportunity to do so yet. At this point she was still a sports reporter rather than a broadcaster. How she would enjoy, she often thought, traveling with the Vikings or another major team, broadcasting for their entire season. That was still to come, but come it would. With her strong voice and flair for drama Nickie realized she could bat out a story in a matter of minutes at the ball park.

People go to watch games for the fun of it. If they can't go, they watch television or listen to their car radio in the hope of some entertainment. Nickie was well aware of that and expended a great deal of effort in making her air time as enjoyable as possible. If she were to broadcast, she dreamed, she would never spice her words with clichés. She would always call the plays exactly as she saw them, and if a batter looked to her as if he were playing to the grandstands instead of to his team, she would never miss telling the world about it in no uncertain terms. Unlike some in the profession, she would be scrupulously honest. In her reporting now her descriptions were precise, her comments wry, and her aim to entertain, even to irritate, but above all, never to bore. She had succeeded and would, she was determined, rise to even greater heights. She knew Ruthanne had told the truth about the soaring ratings the station had won, but she also knew that a lot of powerful people had been irritated by her insistence upon no-nonsense, no-gloss reporting, and by her insistence upon airing her philosophy of sports. Metz was one of the people she irritated. Though that made her a little uncomfortable, she shrugged it off, thinking of him as an old toad who never stopped croaking.

It was a little more difficult making her report amusing when she had only prelisted facts and figures to work from as today, but she managed to glean an interesting angle from the pages in front of her and fashion it into a good report.

Bidding her listeners a jaunty good-bye, she tucked her shirttails back in her pants and prepared to plan for the coveted interview she had this week with the new manager of the Los Angeles team who, by a stroke of good fortune, was planning a trip to Seattle. She had read of the trip a few weeks ago and had prevailed upon him by phone and letter to grant her this interview. When he agreed she was understandably triumphant, for this interview was to be the first bit of direct contact anybody in the state of Washington was to have with an important competitor in the next season. She made a beeline for her office where she closeted herself for the next two hours, polishing and repolishing her planned interview with the Los Angeles manager and going over preliminary notes for tomorrow's show.

On her way out later that evening she routinely checked her mailbox. There was nothing unusual except a note from Metz summoning her to a four o'clock meeting in his office. Nickie grimaced, for she avoided Metz whenever possible. She would think about it tomorrow, for now she was looking forward to a good, long night's sleep.

Though she dragged her heels a bit Nickie did not actually dread this meeting with Metz. If she didn't look straight at him when he flashed his toothy smiles and didn't listen with full attention to his whiney voice as he complained about this or that she would get through it with her lunch intact, she thought.

Metz was abrupt. He did nothing to spare her feelings. "I'm giving you notice. Fifteen minutes. And don't worry about that interview with Campbell. It's been taken care of."

Nickie felt as if she had been struck a blow. Her hands turned clammy, and she felt cold all over. Her ears felt as though someone had stuffed them up with cotton and her lips refused to form words. She simply stared at Metz, her eyes wide with horror. He looked at her in disgust.

"Cat got your tongue?"

Rage engulfed her and with the rage Nickie found her voice. "What are you talking about? You can't fire me! Nobody's ever done a better job and you know it!"

"I'm the boss here, and don't you tell me what I can do. You're through, finished. Do I make myself clear?"

Nickie could tell from the nasal tone of his voice that Metz was enjoying this hugely. She had heard that tone before. It always reminded her of bratty kids thumbing their nose at someone with a singsong *nah, nah, nah.*

"And what do you mean that interview has been taken care of? That's my baby. I planned it and set it up!"

"Your replacement has done it in your stead. Taped it in L.A. It was more convenient all around."

"That's piracy, Stan Metz! And on what grounds are you firing me?"

"Dislike, Nickie." He uttered the words with a studied blandness. "In addition to which, you're opinionated. You can't just stick to the scores, always having to put your two cents in. That's the trouble with you women. You get too emotional."

Nickie controlled herself with an effort. "Those aren't grounds. It won't wash, and as far as I'm concerned I still have my job." She was bluffing and she feared he knew it. She certainly was in no position to make a federal case of it if she did lose her job.

Gleefully rubbing his hands together, Metz showed his trump card.

"There's also the small matter of a missed radio report."

"You can't be serious. I never missed a day. Why I even worked when I was laid up, sick at home." Nickie's well-modulated voice had risen an octave.

Metz looked at her with an ill-concealed smirk. As if the curtain had lifted, Nickie suddenly saw what had happened.

"Is it by any chance the Chicago game that you claim I missed?"

"That's the one, Chickee. When there was silence from your end of the hookup, we had to use our Chicago affiliate's report. Lucky we were able to clear it with them fast."

Nickie sucked in her cheeks, "You set me up." She shook her head disbelievingly. "I thought that offer of a telephone hookup was too nice coming from you. Well, it looks like you won this round, *Mr.* Metz."

It was obvious to her that she was impotent in this situation. It was his word against hers, and he had seniority and a managerial position. Metz raised his eyebrows arrogantly. Nickie turned and walked briskly to her office. Feeling as though she had just been mugged, she sat immobile at her desk. Though she was sorely tempted to complain to the higher-ups, she knew that was impossible. It would be considered insubordination. Organization people don't accuse colleagues even if they are rat finks. She would be the loser either way.

There was a knock at her door. Ruthanne stood there, the picture of dejection.

"I know what happened. I wanted to warn you, but

there was nothing I could do to stop him. When you were out sick he interviewed Jack Knowles for your job. Flew him out from Los Angeles. It was in the bag. He was just waiting for a reasonable excuse to do you in. I'm sorry. I couldn't bring myself to tell you."

Nickie thought she saw a glint of tears in her friend's eyes. She swallowed the lump in her own throat. All her hopes and dreams dashed! Oh, where was Craig now? She had to talk to him. He would be able to help her get things straight.

Excusing herself from a desolate Ruthanne, Nickie dialed Craig's number. She was in luck, for he was at home, and sensing the urgency of her request, promised to meet her in the lobby of the radio station in ten minutes.

When he arrived Nickie was sitting huddled in a corner, shivering despite the seventy-two-degree temperature.

"Hey, what's the matter?" He raised her chin to look into her anguish-filled eyes.

She poured out her story, emphasizing Stan Metz's treatment of her from the beginning. Not wanting to complain and having actually dismissed Metz's nitpicking as irrelevant, she hadn't mentioned it before to Craig. As he listened to her narrative, Craig's face became suffused with fury. He clenched and unclenched his powerful fists convulsively. His lips were drawn into a grim line. She leaned toward him, needing to feel his strong arms around her. He drew her close. She nestled her head against the sleek muscles of his broad chest and laid her hand over the mat of curling black hairs which peeked out from the top of his shirt. She felt safe.

"There's a chance I could appeal," she stammered. "The top brass at the station might support me."

His arms tightened around her. "You're not going back

there begging! And I'm not going to have you working with that guy Metz again. I ought to wipe the floor with him."

"Don't do anything like that. Please!" She was alarmed and feeling vaguely uncomfortable at this turn of events. She wasn't used to playing damsel in distress to someone else's knight in shining armor. Although, she had to laugh at herself, it would be nice to see Stan Metz flattened!

"What are you laughing about?"

"Nothing." She paused. "Maybe this is the shove I needed. I can go to a bigger city and look for a bigger job. Job-hopping is the way to success anyway."

"That depends on the way you define success," Craig answered, loosening his grip on her at the same time. "But I've got a better solution. Wait here while I make a call."

Nickie let herself drop to a bench, where she sat hunched over, chin in hands. Craig was back in a matter of minutes, his demeanor visibly brightened.

"You've got an interview at WLDJ. I'll drive you over in my car."

"The television station! How did you manage that?"

"I know the producer of *Sportswatch.* He mentioned a couple of days ago that their sportscaster/reporter just up and announced his departure. They've got the broadcasting fairly well covered from within the ranks but are looking around for a reporter with some broadcasting experience. I don't believe they've made the opening public yet. He knows your work and was pretty interested when I told him you were available. I'd guess you've got a good shot at it."

Nickie opened her eyes wide and laughed out loud with happiness. But her laughter died abruptly when she looked down at her attire, wrinkled khaki jeans and quilted patchwork vest.

"I can't go for an interview dressed like this. And I don't have an up-to-date résumé. I think I have a tape I had made of myself at the bottom of this bag, though. I'm sure I do. I have everything else in here. One day, over the rainbow, I'll clean it out."

"You'll do great. Don't worry," Craig said confidently. Nickie wasn't as sure of the outcome as Craig seemed to be. She was a disoriented bundle of nerves when Craig dropped her in front of the television studio. He made her promise to meet him at the pub on the corner when she was finished.

The pub was crowded with earnest, slow-talking men, mostly Boeing engineers. Heads turned to stare at her as a flushed and sparkling-eyed Nickie entered through the stone archway. Her exotic, careless good looks were in stark contrast to most of the women there with their blond lacquered beauty and monogrammed sweaters. Spotting her immediately, Craig stood up. She weaved her way through the crowded floor unaware of men who ogled or women who gave her a quick once-over.

"I got it! Oh, Craig, I can't believe how well this has worked out!"

"I'm not surprised," he said with equanimity. "I knew you'd get the job."

"I wasn't so sure." She lowered her eyes. "There's a lot of hard competition for something like this, and granted I'm not bad at what I do, I am fairly new to it." Nickie thought it a shame that she was too modest to say what she really felt, that she knew she was the best and she was glad the producer was smart enough to see it!

Craig leaned back in his chair with his arms folded across his chest.

"I knew Quinn," he named the producer, "would come through. He owed me one."

Nickie's mouth fell open at his words, which struck like poison-tipped arrows. How to deflate someone's ego with ten easy words, she thought.

"I think I had a little something to do with it too," she whispered.

He flashed her a heart-melting smile. "Of course you did. Everyone could use a little help from their friends, that's all. What are you having to drink?"

"A glass of white wine will be fine."

Craig tipped his head back and swallowed the remains of his Jack Daniel's. He crooked his eyebrow at the waitress, who hurried over as if she had gotten a royal summons.

"Fill this up for me, sweetheart, and a champagne cocktail for the lady."

Nickie bit her bottom lip in vexation.

"We're celebrating. Nobody celebrates with plain old white wine," he explained.

"Then why did you bother asking me?" she snapped.

For the second time that day Nickie felt her spirits plummet. First she had lost her job and then she had lost her dignity. What in the world was happening to her? She used to be strong and capable. Then she had met Craig. Where before she would have handled the loss of her job, now her first thought had been to seek the comfort of his arms, to run to him. But on the other hand, she brooded, what an ungrateful wretch she was. He had gone out on a limb to get her this interview, and now she was to start a far better job. But, she warred with herself, all he did was get her the interview. *She* had gotten the job. He had no right to act smug and condescending! And then to order champagne when she asked for wine! Sometimes the deepest of feelings were unmasked in the most trivial of incidents. Undoubtedly he thought she was fun and probably sexy, but he had to know there was much more to her than that!

"Relax," he said expansively as he pushed his chair back to accommodate outstretched legs.

Nickie guessed that he was enjoying the situation. She remembered, in the dim past, overhearing someone bitterly complain that it was easier to grant a favor than to receive one. She knew now what had been meant.

Oblivious to Nickie's disgruntled state of mind Craig spoke in a dreamy voice. "The season's almost over. Why don't we go away together when it's done? I could use a vacation. Someplace quiet. Maybe the Caribbean. How about it? Just you and me and white sand and piña coladas."

"I'm sorely tempted, but I'm just starting a new job, remember? Why don't you go without me though?"

"Surely you could arrange something. I'll talk to Quinn about it."

"Not this time," she said firmly, "although the thought of hot sand, clear water, and nothing in my head except should I wear my black maillot or my white bikini is almost enough to make me change my mind. But not quite."

"*Achhh!*" he groaned. "The work ethic is ruining this country. What's left to a man when his favorite girl chooses work over play?"

"He could play with his second favorite girl," Nickie teased.

"Said creature doesn't exist." Craig held up his hands. 'But perhaps I should remedy the situation," he said, teasing.

As if on cue, a curvacious blonde in white pants that looked as though they had been spray-painted on, sidled over to their table. "Why, if it isn't Craig Boone! I'm honored. I don't mind saying you're my very favorite baseball player," she gushed.

"Why, thank you, ma'am," Craig said, half standing in acknowledgment.

The blonde glanced back at her table where two friends stared at the scenario with an air of ill-concealed expectation. Nickie correctly guessed that they had probably placed bets on the outcome of her forthcoming pitch. She also sized it up as a screwball, and as she waited with about as much anticipation as the blonde's friends, she amused herself with her unspoken puns. She was not disappointed.

The blonde whipped a green felt tip pen. "You don't mind giving me your autograph, do you?"

"For your nephew, right?" Craig said, and laughed.

"Not exactly." She bent over and turned a ripe-looking derriere in Craig's direction. "Right there'll do fine," she simpered, patting her back pocket. "Kind of like you'll be branding me," she cooed.

Nickie pinched her sides to keep from laughing. So this is what fame got you! She had to admit that Craig handled the girl with remarkable aplomb when he signed a cocktail napkin, tucked it in her back pocket, and regretfully told her that he could only write on a flat surface. The girl tittered her thanks and rejoined her astonished friends.

Craig took one look at Nickie and mistook the meaning

of the poker face which she wore. "Hey, it's not my fault. I can't help it if the girl wants to make an ass of herself!"

"C'mon," she said, and laughed, her good humor restored. "You loved every minute!" She looked up at him with doe eyes. "Oh, Craig," she mimicked the blonde's breathless tones, "it'll be just like you're branding me!"

"It sounds better coming from you," he bantered. "It wouldn't *look* bad on you either. With a nice tan from that Caribbean vacation I was trying to lure you on."

Nickie stopped laughing. Although Craig's words were jocular, there was a stony expression in his eyes and a pulsating nerve in his jaw which told her that he was more disturbed by her refusal to join him than he let on.

She swallowed hard. "It sounds great, really. But I . . ."

He held up his hand. "Say no more. Will you have another glass of champagne?"

"Please." Nickie drained the remaining half of her glass in one swallow. "Speaking of invitations, can you come with me to Ruthanne's tomorrow night? She's planned a small party to celebrate their final mortgage payment. I meant to ask you sooner, but what with one thing and another it completely slipped my mind." Her words tripped over each other.

"Tomorrow night, eh?" Craig's voice reminded her of a long, soft drawl which, for a born and bred northwesterner, would have made her laugh in another circumstance. "I can't. I'm tied up. Even when I'm not playing I've got things I have to do. Sorry."

"Oh."

"One refusal has nothing to do with the other," he added, guessing her thoughts.

"Of course not," she said a trifle too quickly. "We both

110

have lives, other obligations. I can go to Ruthanne's alone." She wasn't sure how to read the look on his face. "You want to get me to the Caribbean very badly, don't you?" Craig leaned very close to her. He stared at her mouth. She caught his scent, an expensive cologne mixed with a male muskiness impossible to disguise. The golden amber lights of his eyes flashed mockingly at her, and she knew she had to be flip, for what she saw in his gaze was raw hunger. As her own glance took in the way his light cotton shirt caressed the hard muscles of his chest and arms as he leaned forward, an answering flame of desire licked at her own insides. She imagined him naked beside her, his body lean, taut, and beautiful. She thought she must be crazy to be thinking this way after all that had happened today. And then his eyes dropped to her breasts making her ache for his touch, and she realized with terrifying clarity that she was, despite all her will, powerless against this man.

"I want to make love to you very badly," he corrected. She thought his breath ragged under the well-modulated voice.

"Shall we go?" He stood up, indicating that his question was more in the nature of a command.

She nodded mutely and followed him out to his car.

Sitting in the passenger seat, she thought that he was so sure of himself that he had not even the courtesy to ask the proverbial "your place or mine?" She certainly wasn't going to ask. She would find out soon enough. The slight pressure of his hand on her knee made her legs tremble, an involuntary response which Nickie did her utmost to control.

"What is it that keeps you so busy those nights ve

mentioned?" she murmured, more in an effort to appear casual than out of a desire to pry.

"Things I'm involved in," he answered evasively.

Nickie shot him a sidelong glance. *What things?* her thoughts screamed out.

Instead, she laughed off his secrecy. "This isn't an I.R.S. audit, you know."

The pale moon followed the car as it hummed through quiet streets. After about five minutes Nickie surmised that it was to her apartment that they were headed. During the forty-five-minute ride she tried to think of amusing, witty things to say. It astonished her that she drew a blank. She was conscious only of his big hands, one of which rested lightly on the steering wheel, the other remaining on her knee. What was wrong with her? This wasn't Nickie Alexander. Okay, she was going to make love with him, but this wouldn't be the first time. She was a grown woman, so why was she breathless with anticipation? And why, as she sat in a leather car seat, did her body tremble.

Her questions remained unanswered. As she pressed the button for her elevator, fished out her keys, and once inside, hung up his camel sports coat, she felt like a character in an unknown play. She had no will of her own; her lines were already written.

"Come here, lady." Full of assurance he pulled her against him. His arms went around her and she knew the strength of his desire. Her hands passed lightly over the breadth of his back, over his shoulders, and across his chest. She stopped at the place where she felt his mmering beneath her fingertips and fleetingly lips to the spot. He tilted her chin upwards, he could catch his look, which bespoke

112

volumes, his mouth covered hers with a kiss fervent yet tender. He slipped his hand down around her waist and led her into her own bedroom. Feeling like the only woman in the world, like an irresistible goddess, aware not only of his power over her but of hers over him, she waited for him to disrobe her. She stood before him, and his eyes never once left her face as, with deliberate slowness, he unbuttoned her blouse. She let it lie where it dropped at her feet. He tore his gaze from hers and lowered it to her breasts. She was lucky, she knew, that her firm bosom needed little help, for she favored the flimsiest of undergarments.

"Nicole," he said huskily as his hands met to unsnap elasticized lace.

Nickie noticed the adeptness with which he divested her of her bra, and the unbidden thought that these were much practiced hands sprang into her mind.

Her soft breasts, which appeared all the larger for the contrast with her slender frame, tumbled into his waiting hands. Warm lips grazed the hollow of her throat and moved with tantalizing slowness over the rounded curves which presented themselves to him. Nickie could not suppress a moan of pleasure. His hands roamed all over her body, divesting her in one rapid movement of her silk panties. As she closed her eyes, she felt him lift her up to deposit her gently on the bed. She opened her eyes to watch the ritual of his undressing. He was arrogantly unselfconscious, standing there towering above her. She could almost feel the curling black hairs that spread out like a fan over his wide chest and disappeared in a line beneath his belt before he was totally naked and stretched out next to her, flattening her own soft curves against his lean hardness. Every nerve in her body reveled in this

113

contact with his skin, longed for his passionate kisses, for his hot breath against her mouth. As he moved to join her, he caught her wrists with one hand and drew them over her head. He kissed her then, a kiss fiery and long, a drugging kiss to stir a passion long since ignited.

From her mouth his kisses forged a smoldering trail over the curves of her breast, her hips, the slight swell of her belly to her slim thighs. His dark eyes were smoky as he surveyed the form that was beneath him now.

"I need to be with you, Nicole. You're becoming a habit after only one time."

Her eyes sought his, wanting to hear more.

"Don't say anything," he commanded as he plundered the inner recesses of her mouth.

Had she wanted to she couldn't have uttered a word, so swept along by desire and sensuous abandon was she. She lost all sense of time as she savored his touch and the feel of his smooth skin and throbbing muscles. He looked and felt to her almost savagely masculine. Her hands caressed his back in massaging circles, and she could barely restrain herself from pleading with him to enter her as he prolonged their lovemaking with delicious explorations. When finally they came together, their bodies fit perfectly, like a real-life vision of a master sculptor. Her mind was a blank; all that existed was the exquisite pleasure of him that she wanted to last and last. And yet when their passion exploded in the intense heat of fulfillment, and she soared with him to its heights, she knew a moment of absolute oneness with this man that was beyond anything she had ever before experienced. She had to bite her lip to keep from screaming that she loved him. His words as they reached the zenith were incomprehensible. It didn't matter. His body spoke clearly enough.

Afterwards as they lay in the tangled bedsheets, their moist bodies not touching, he smiled at her so sweetly and tenderly that it made her heart lurch.

She watched his naked form retreat into the bathroom and thought that Michelangelo could not have conceived of more beautiful a male physique. With lines that were straight, lean yet muscled, his proportions were closer to a god's than a mortal's. Baseball players, unlike football players, didn't have to be big. Craig, at six foot one and one hundred and eighty pounds, was the exception rather than the rule. She thought that most other men that size would have crushed her beneath their bulk. Craig, however, knew how to handle his body. And hers, she sighed contentedly.

As she heard the shower in the bathroom stop running, she wrapped herself in a sheet and gathered her night things. On second thought, she replaced the filmy beige negligee she had chosen for the red Vikings nightshirt Craig had given her.

The bathroom door opened and Craig reappeared, a towel wrapped around his waist. His black curls, still damp from a cursory towel drying, clung to his neck.

"That's how I first saw you," Nickie murmured.

"You should have been warned. It was an omen of things to come!"

"Exquisite things," Nickie responded lightly as she brushed past him for her own shower.

She turned the hot water on full blast, and as steam filled the room, she glanced at herself in the mirror. Her hair was disheveled, her lips had a poutish, thoroughly kissed look, and her eyes gleamed with a mix of insolence and satiety. She felt great, she thought as her image misted over.

Craig was fully dressed when she emerged.

"It's ten o'clock and we haven't eaten. I'm going to bring back some dinner from the house. I just called Jo-Jo. He'll have it ready."

An hour later, Craig was back with a thinly sliced London Broil, a Caesar salad, and Julienne potatoes. Nickie dined immodestly in the red nightshirt. She was not unaware of the way it heightened the flush in her cheeks or of its brilliant contrast with the dark halo of curls which surrounded her face.

"I've never cooked for you," she remarked suddenly.

"You'll have to remedy that next time. Are you a good cook?"

"When I'm motivated."

"I'm motivated . . . but not to cook." He looked at her meaningfully.

"Give a girl a break!" She laughed. "I'm not even finished with my salad!"

"I want you to work up a hearty appetite." He pulled her to her feet and led her back to the bedroom where he commenced to make glorious love to her again and again.

CHAPTER TEN

The next morning as Nickie opened sleepy eyes she smiled to herself. The aroma of fresh coffee and sizzling bacon assailed her nostrils.

"Smells good," she shouted through a yawn.

Craig appeared at the doorway with spatula in hand.

"I'm a man of many talents."

"So I've noticed. But I was going to do the cooking next."

"I didn't want to wake you, and I've got excess energy to burn."

"Still" she teased. "I do have to admit that I've always dreamed of waking up and finding my coffee ready and waiting. I'm practically in a coma till that first cup. You might be worth keeping around!"

"It just might be worth sticking around!" he said with a sly grin.

"I hope that's not a leer I see!" She slid back under the covers. "I think I'm going back to sleep."

"I'll be waiting in the kitchen. At this moment the bacon is too much for me to resist."

As soon as she heard that he had left the room, Nickie jumped up, ran into the bathroom, where she took a quick shower, brushed her teeth, and swept her hair into a knot on top of her head. She pulled on a pair of tight black denim jeans and her best blouse, a billowy Adolfo red, which although a trifle dressy could not be surpassed for the subtle way it brought out the best of her coloring and figure.

"Good morning," she said as she poured herself a cup of her rich Colombian brew.

Craig looked at her speculatively. "You're a vision to send a man's pulse a-racing."

He set a plate of fried eggs and bacon in front of her and sat opposite her with the mountain of food he had piled on his own plate. Nickie smiled broadly for no reason other than sheer joy. Not having known that love could be so easy, the delight she felt was indeed a revelation.

"Delicious!" she pronounced after her first mouthful. "Not that I didn't expect it to be!"

Craig scraped back his chair as he reached for his second cup of coffee. His proportions seemed too large for her small apartment. Her breakfast table scaled for one person seemed like a toy in front of him. She had the feeling that a less graceful man would have been bumping and banging into cupboards and counters.

"Do you have practice this afternoon?"

"Mm-hmm, at two o'clock."

"Good. That means you have the morning free. What shall we do?" Nickie's voice bubbled over. She was never one for concealing her emotions. "There's a marvelous exhibit at the Oriental Museum."

"Let's wait awhile on that. They're going to have something on the history of baseball in Japan soon."

"Okay. Sounds great. Maybe I could do something with that for the show."

118

"It's a deal. Besides, I can't go this morning anyway. I'm going sky diving."

Nickie felt as though she'd been dashed with cold water.

"Excuse me? I thought you said sky diving." She gave a nervous laugh.

"I did. I have a lesson at ten o'clock."

"Please don't go."

"What?" It was Craig's turn to be surprised. "Why shouldn't I go? I'll try anything once," he said, and laughed.

"It's dangerous." Nickie felt like a fool even as she uttered the words. She looked down at her plate with its two sunshine-perfect yolks and crisp bacon. Where before she had been ravenous, now even the faintest stirring of hunger were gone. The food on Craig's plate had disappeared, and he was buttering several slices of toast as he listened to Nickie with a puzzled expression on his face. He chewed slowly. Nickie had felt the blood drain from her face and knew she was pale as snow.

"There's nothing to worry about," he said after a while. Pushing back her chair, Nickie ran from the table to stand at her bay window. Maybe if she pushed everything from her head and concentrated on Mount Rainier, she would regain her composure. Her legs felt rubbery and she suspected that were she a tightly cosseted eighteenth-century damsel she would have fainted.

"There's nothing to worry about, little one." The words repeated themselves in her consciousness—the last words her father had spoken to her on a long-ago day, almost twenty years before, as he left with her mother to embark on that ill-fated plane trip. Ghosts of childhood sorrow rushed back at her, and Nickie didn't even know that tears were streaming down her cheeks. Craig whirled her around. She hadn't heard him behind her.

Exasperation showed plainly around his mouth. "Does it start already, the Inquisition? My God, I thought you were different!" He spoke harshly. "You, the independent career woman! You're like every other namby-pamby lady out there waiting to put a yoke around a man's neck and harness him to her bedpost! Well I'm having none of it! Nobody's going to manipulate me, tears or not! And I thought you were smarter, or more subtle, at any rate. But no, you started out with a zinger! I guess I'm lucky at that. Because *nobody* tells me what I can or can't do. I've been that route already!"

Each word sounded like a shot in her ears. She was as if paralyzed by sound. She was sickened, for she knew that if she were he, she might have spoken the same words. She didn't turn around as she heard him stomp out or even when she heard the doorjamb crack with the force of his slam. The door opened a second later and he was back.

"Do you have any wood cement? It looks like I cracked your door."

"No, I don't. But don't worry about it," she said acerbically. "What's one security deposit more or less?"

Why couldn't she say what she really felt? she berated herself. What was it they said about foolish pride? Craig was right. She *had* been manipulative, and though he hadn't said it, hysterical as well. Yes, her parents had been killed in a plane, but it was about time she got over her fears. If she were to be a big broadcasting star, she would have to fly all over the country. CBS or NBC wouldn't be sending her to the World Series via Greyhound!

"I'm going downstairs to borrow some from the super. I'll be right up."

120

"Suit yourself," she answered in a neutral tone. Well, he *had* overreacted, she ruminated indignantly. There was no reason for him to explode. Was she supposed to fall all over him just because he returned with hung head?

Craig had the wood cement in hand when he came up. He applied it methodically, let it dry, and tested the door to his satisfaction.

"As good as new," he pronounced. "I think I'll finish my breakfast now. Do you want to pop some new bread in the toaster while I wash my hands?"

"Sure." She sat down, poured herself another cup of coffee, and idly pushed eggs around her plate. Grease had congealed around the edges of cold bacon, and despite good intentions she found herself unable to eat.

How could he be so calm? she wondered as she watched him spread butter and red currant jelly on his toast. Annoyed with him as she was, she could not help but feel a bit guilty when she remembered that she had never gotten around to making jam out of the blueberries they had picked. "Did I ever tell you about my ex-wife?" he suddenly asked.

"A little . . . Don't you remember?"

"Oh, yes. I always try to forget when I talk about her," he snorted. "One of her more aggravating traits was that she had to know exactly where I was. She even checked the odometer to make sure my stories checked out mileage-wise. I would have had more freedom in a federal penitentiary. Ironic, since she was the one who split. But that marriage wouldn't have lasted long anyway."

"Is that by way of a warning?"

"No, it's by way of an explanation. You're special to me, Nicole. Real special. I'm just a little gun-shy."

He stood up and stretched. "What's the matter? Don't

you like my cooking?" He looked pointedly at Nickie's full plate.

"Your cooking's fine. I'm not terribly hungry this morning."

"I hope you're not watching your weight. I like a woman with a hearty appetite. And your pounds seem to go to the right places."

Nickie smiled dolefully. "I'll try to do better next time."

"You're not still mad, are you?"

"There's nothing to be mad about." Nickie's voice was measured.

"Good. I'd better get going."

"Have fun." Nickie could not keep the dryness out of her voice.

"I'll call you later. Have a good time at Ruthanne's."

Nickie had a terrible foreboding that he would not return after he walked out the door this time. She stood still, looking at the mended door, a hairline crack still visible despite the wood cement.

"I'll give you a call later," his voice resounded in her mind.

"Don't worry, little one," her father had said.

I'll call you later, don't worry, little one, I'll call you later. . . . Nickie trembled. She ran into her bedroom, tearing off her bright red blouse as she went. She was cold and not in a red mood. She pulled an old black turtleneck over her head. As she caught a glimpse of her white, drawn face, her hollow eyes, and tight-lipped mouth in the mirror she had to laugh. Perhaps she had missed her calling. She was marvelous at melodrama and should have been a soap opera star! That was, she perceived, one of the reasons she had kept herself in tight control these last years. She could, if she allowed it, be very emotional,

122

maudlin even. But she didn't like herself that way. She preferred distancing herself from anybody or anything that could wring tears from her. She had had enough of pain and sorrow as a youngster to last a lifetime. Relationships were fine—as long as they gave her what she wanted from them but not when they took what she didn't want to give. Craig was dangerous to her. She had sensed that when first she saw him. Long ago she had learned that her intuition was to be trusted.

It wasn't only with people that she guarded her emotions like fragile antique lace; she carefully chose her reading matter. Usually it was nonfiction that she read, or if fiction, she checked first to make sure the ending was happy. She chose the movies she saw by the reviews, never going in blind. Once she had been put upon by a friend to see a film about an Indian family, a sad and tragic tale of kidnapping and death and fruitless search. She had been haunted by the film for days after. This was a side of herself which Nickie went to great pains to hide. Besides her desire for strength and independence, Nickie did not find hysterical women very admirable characters. These thoughts and others passed through her mind as she faced herself in the mirror.

Well, since she had no intention of pacing back and forth, scanning the horizon for signs of Craig's plane, she thought she might as well do something constructive. Since she was about to start a new job, she decided to spend some time today cleaning out her desk at WRPJ.

As she left the sanctuary of her apartment for the radio station, she prayed that she would not run into Stan Metz. He was more than she could take today.

She was not to be spared.

123

"Good morning, Nickie," Metz said silkily as she entered the auspices of Ruthanne's outer office.

Nickie nodded curtly. Ruthanne was nowhere to be seen, alas.

"I heard that you landed the job at WLDJ. It pays to have friends in the right places."

Nickie shrugged. She refused, she swore silently, to be sucked into conversation with that creep. Moving swiftly to the small office, cubicle really, which housed her desk, she was annoyed to hear the swish of polyester trouser legs behind her. She breathed a sigh of relief as she stood in her old office. Her crowded desk with its piles of papers, memos, and half-bitten pencils did not look like the desk of someone recently fired. She moved to close the door. As she should have guessed, Metz, sallow-complexioned and beady-eyed, stood in the doorway watching her. Though she felt a tug of nostalgia looking at the desk which had been hers for so short a time, not wanting to afford Metz undue pleasure, she wiped all expression from her face.

"Cleaning out the ol' desk, eh? Make sure you leave the stapler and scotch tape where you found 'em. Heh, heh, just a little joke."

Nickie rolled her eyes upward. Every cloud had a silver lining. In this case it was platinum—a teriffic new job and the last of Stan Metz!

Still, Nickie didn't answer.

"What's the matter?" Metz's voice turned surly. "Cat got your tongue? I'll bet you're not so quiet with that Casanova boyfriend of yours!"

Nickie faced him with an icy glare.

"Do you remember what Bo McGraw said when he refused to fight Tiger Henderson?" Nickie asked sweetly.

"Can't say that I do."

"He said, 'it's not worth my while. I might soil my boxing gloves on his greasy, fat head.' "

Metz jumped back, and as she closed the door in his astonished face she heard him sputtering outraged deprecations. Ruthanne would enjoy this story, Nickie chuckled.

Bending over, she busied herself with her desk. Innumerable papers were discarded. All she kept were research notes and tapes of her broadcasts. Not until she was finished with her task did Metz's words fully register.

I'll bet you're not so quiet with that Casanova boyfriend of yours, he had said. Nickie sank into the swivel chair behind the desk. What exactly did he mean by that? Everyone knew Metz was privy to some of the best gossip in the sports world. Was he now being viciously inventive? Or *was* Craig a Casanova of sorts? What was unquestionably true, Nickie decided after a dizzying few minutes, was that she was becoming unhinged. Suspicions, doubts, and fears were taking over a once calmly forceful personality. If this is what love did, who needed it?

Love, it was a word that meant so many different things to people. Nickie set her mouth in a purposeful line. To this person it would mean only one thing, happiness. The goblins must be put to rest. Jealousy and fears must not be permitted to consume her. She was her own woman. And it was that brazen, confident woman who had enchanted Craig, not some sniveling weakling. Granted, Craig had been a bit harsh in what he had said to her, but he had been right. If—Nickie took a deep breath at the thought—he wanted to jump out of planes, then let him jump! She would be his lover but not his keeper. As she framed the thought in her mind the sense of freedom and serenity which had been sorely lacking of late was hers again. She would go to Craig! She would be there as his plane landed to tell him it was all right! Theirs would be a love free and pure. They would laugh and eat raspberries and cream in the woods and walk along the waterfront in the rain and make beautiful, endless love. They would be together and they would be apart. They would be able to be themselves. And when they argued, as all lovers must, it would be about the most frivolous of things, such as which movie to see or which star shone brightest in the sky. Nickie smiled. There was no time for regrets in this life—it was far too short.

Clutching her bulging briefcase, she looked calmly around the office before she left. This small office, and she hadn't really had the time to get to know it. She sighed. That's the way it went sometimes. She was off to bigger things.

Noticing the light which burned dimly in Metz's office, Nickie grinned triumphantly. He was certain to remain holed up in there until she had left. Perhaps she should have practiced the venerable art of insult earlier. Her natural good manners had precluded that possibility. They had, in fact, presented one of her biggest impediments as a reporter. She often felt a nagging discomfiture when asking the probing, digging questions of athletes that were central to her profession. That she overcame it was due to an even more powerful urge to succeed.

"Good-bye, WRPJ," she sang out as the elevator door opened for her. "Good-bye, Mr. Metz, and good riddance!"

The brisk air felt good on her face as she walked the block to her car. She threw her briefcase in the backseat, gunned the motor like a cocky adolescent, and nosed her car in the direction of the airport. Last night had been lovely. Surely she would be forgiven one morning's brief aberration of spirit. Full of goodwill, full of herself, Nickie was not affected by the association it held for her when she pulled into the airport's parking lot. It had been years since she had been here. She had become something of an expert at circumventing invitations to bon voyage parties or requests for rides from friends or acquaintances. The mere mention of the airport never failed to conjure up images of her parents that she preferred to forget. It made her glad that she was not now seized by familiar sensations. It was the present that occupied her thoughts and not the past. She was bent on seeing Craig and on telling him why she had come.

She entered the terminal by the exit nearest to her. A pleasant young woman behind the Northwest counter directed her to the furthest end of the airport, which was used for small, private planes. Though it was a veritable hike to get there, Nickie didn't mind. The clean-shaven businessmen with their matter-of-fact airs, the porters bustling with loaded cars, the news vendors chewing on their cigars as they pocketed dollars and quarters, made her realize how silly she had been. Planes were a fact of life and the worst of accidents could happen in one's own kitchen. She looked down at the black turtleneck and black jeans she was wearing. How utterly inappropriate, she thought. Little did she know that not a male pair of eyes passed by without riveting upon her. With her red lips and cheeks, her black hair curled out like a mane, and her black outfit, she looked like the most alluring, daring, and bohemian of creatures. When finally she arrived at the small cinder block terminal where Craig was to debark, she was relieved, upon asking the clerk to check his computer printout, to learn that he was due in within the next fifteen minutes.

She sat on one of the plastic chairs which proliferate in airline terminals, facing a plate glass wall. From that vantage point, she was able to view the entire runway. It was a clear day, not even a wisp of a cloud to be seen. She watched planes taking off and landing and even suffered vicarious abdominal butterflies at especially bumpy landings. This was not uninteresting, she mused. And were she not here for an express purpose, would not be a bad way to while away a Saturday afternoon.

Craig's plane was ten minutes late. It was a ten minutes which, though she was aware of the seconds ticking by, did not send her into a tailspin of worry. When she heard the words, "That's the plane you're waiting for, miss," she smiled gratefully and thought it nice that people actually could outgrow their fears. She had suspected that personal growth and change were myths invented by newspaper columnists for optimistic, post–front-page breakfast-time reading.

She stood up, her nose pressed against the glass, eager to greet Craig. The propeller of the two-seater was still whirring when the door swung open. Craig stepped jauntily down the metal stairway and waited for the companion who followed behind. He placed an arm around the slender shoulders of the petite blonde who smiled up at him. His expression, as he looked at the petulantly pretty thirty-five-plus face, was earnest. Nickie's vision blurred. Jumping back from the window, she ran to the ladies' room just beyond the gate. She had seen enough and did not want herself to be seen.

Gripping the white porcelain sink, she looked at herself in a metal-rimmed mirror. What she saw there was the stricken look of someone who had been thoroughly and finally disillusioned. Where a few minutes ago her color had been high, now a chalky pallor made her look ill.

What a fool she had been. The most she could say for herself was that she had been relatively discreet. Unlike most other media people she knew, she kept her private life under wraps. That her romantic debacle was a private affair provided precious little comfort as she stood there rooted to the tile floor, her knuckles turning almost as white as the sink she grasped. And the most she could say for Craig Boone, she thought with undaunted wryness, was that he had boundless energy. Yes, that man was truly an athlete!

Then a small voice at the back of her mind reproved her for jumping to conclusions. She had been known to be wrong before. Wasn't it just possible that there was a perfectly innocent explanation? And wasn't it just possible, her more cynical voice nagged, that little green men had populated the earth three thousand years ago and were at this very moment using a giant telescope to write an intergalactic best seller on human civilization? She couldn't stay here forever looking at those big, sad eyes in the mirror, she thought, as impatience crowded out pain. She opened the rest room door a slit in order to peek out. A head-on collision with her erstwhile paramour was very much to be avoided.

With his arm still thrown casually over the blond woman's shoulders he was rounding the bend toward the next terminal. Responding to some indefinable urge—on later reflection Nickie decided that it was a throwback to her prefeminist days—Nickie followed the couple. The ease with which she followed him surprised her, and she might even have enjoyed the role of Mata Hari had the circumstances been different. Half expecting Craig to turn around and confront her while she babbled some idiotic excuse, she was relieved when saw them walk to the parking lot still engrossed in conversation. She made for her car. It was parked directly in Craig's line of vision as he walked on. She didn't have much fear that he would recognize it. He was much too intent on the blonde's conversation. Nickie was not, in that particular instance, thrilled at her insight into Craig's nature. One of the things she liked best about him was the feeling that when he was with her he was one hundred percent there. What a pity, she thought angrily, that it was obviously not a feeling unique unto her. From the brief glimpse she had gotten of his face as he exited from the plane, he wouldn't have heard a bomb fall in front of him.

Her heart thumped as she slid in behind the wheel of her Mazda. She put it into gear and drove out around the parking lot. There was a smaller parking area right next to the ramp leading onto the highway. She let her engine idle there while she waited for Craig's shiny Maserati to pass.

As she watched the luxury vehicle whiz by (Craig was not one for obeying posted speed limits), she followed at a safe distance. Out on the road her foot pressed further down on the accelerator than was customary for her. She followed him off at the fifth exit. He was heading toward one of Seattle's scenic inlets. Once on the secondary road Nickie slowed up to allow a yellow Buick to pass. She slid lower in her seat. She could imagine few things more embarrassing than to have him spy her in his rearview mirror as she was spying on him. Gads! she shuddered, what was happening to her? She was acting like a neurotic, jealous wife! Yet she couldn't turn back.

Craig's car was stopped at a red light. Though there were now two other cars separating them, Nickie's eyes searched out Craig and his companion. It looked to her as if he was dabbing at the woman's eyes with a handkerchief. She wondered if it was the monogrammed maroon handkerchief he favored. She had noticed it the first time she saw him pitching because it looked so terribly incongruous hanging half out of the pocket of his baseball uniform. So the woman was crying, she thought. How touching. Perhaps he had told her his heart could not belong to one woman alone or some such nonsense.

Nickie put her head down against the cold steering wheel as a wave of nausea overcame her. With the utmost determination she controlled herself. It would not be polite to throw up in traffic! The honking of the driver behind her made her jump. The light was green and the Maserati was way up the street. When a big semitrailer making an illegal left turn in front of her caused her to lose sight of him, she thought for a frantic moment that she had lost him for good. He was not ahead of her, nor was he on one of the two side streets that she scanned. With a spurt of speed and following a hunch, she turned left toward the water. She was just in time to see the tail end of his unmistakable car taking the next corner. She waited a minute, lest she be seen. When she followed she was in time to see him parking in front of a rickety houseboat, one among dozens moored along the edge of a crystalline inlet.

Craning her neck she watched as he scooted around to the passenger side to help the woman out. At least his manners were intact, she fumed, even if his morals weren't.

Tucking the blonde's arm under his, Craig walked with

131

her to the houseboat and waited while she fished in her oversized pockets for the key. They walked in together. Nickie had seen enough. She wouldn't wait around for the main feature to end. The way Craig operated, she fretted, it would be a long wait.

During the long drive home Nickie's mind was a blank. She drove automatically and if pressed as to the details of the trip would have been at a loss. Feeling numb and like an automaton, she found a parking spot in front of her building, chose the stairs instead of the elevator, and collapsed in her most comfortable chair in front of her favorite view. She found that majestic mountaintops and blue sky were of little help. She wet her lips, for they had grown dry, and put a hand on her pounding heart. Her life, these past couple of days, had been like a roller coaster, and she hated roller coasters. In a matter of hours she had lost and found a job; in a matter of days she had believed she had found the greatest of loves and then that it was all a sham. She had been right about Craig from the beginning. He was not for her. He was a confirmed ladies' man and nothing but trouble. Men like that don't settle down and lead normal lives. They're always after new and bigger kicks in their professional and their personal lives. Hadn't he told her he would try anything? She had taken him cross-country skiing and now the blonde had taken him skydiving. He had taken both of *them* for a ride! Perhaps his next lover would scale the Himalayas with him! What a setup.

At least, she consoled herself, she had found out before it was too late and before she had made a total mess of her life. Nickie didn't like to cast stones, but even though he had helped her get a new job, it had been partly due to him that she had lost WRPJ in the first place. She would never

132

have been so careless as to trip over a tree root or so blind to Metz's machinations had she not been so preoccupied with Craig. And if she didn't watch out she would lose that new job too. A man like Craig Boone, stunning and overpowering, was a danger. For she had too easily lost her heart to him and with it her sense of self. Nickie Alexander didn't rush off like a headless chicken to airports, didn't trail people, and didn't lose control. She didn't create scenes with a man, didn't beg or try to control. Nickie Alexander was free to be herself and to take love where she found it, no strings attached. If and when she found a man who could answer all her needs yet not interfere with her carefully designed life, she would marry. Craig Boone was not that man, and she had been the worst kind of dolt to have entertained the notion that it might work between them. He was a Casanova. Metz had known. That might have been the *only* thing that Metz had ever known.

Their careers would have ridden a collision course anyway. Involved with a pitcher of Craig's stature she would have been denied much of the recognition that was her due. People would naturally assume that only his influence had gotten her where she was. But why was she even thinking these thoughts? What did it matter now? She could never look him in the face again, not after last night. She had surrendered totally to him, had held nothing back, believing that he was hers. What she had witnessed today made a mockery of his sweet kisses. Of course she was not so naive as to expect that one or two passionate escapades between a man and a woman created an unbreakable monogamous bond. But it had been different with them. He had touched a chord in her heart, in her very soul, that she had not known existed. She thought it had been the same for him.

Nickie tried. She paced around her living room. She bit her lip till she drew blood. But she could not stop her tears. To no avail she told herself that Nickie Alexander doesn't cry, as the first flood of tears redoubled. She cried for a Nickie Alexander that didn't exist anymore, and she cried for a Craig that she wouldn't have, not even if he came crawling, which of course he wouldn't do anyway. She cried for the warm comfort of his arms and for the smile that said he knew exactly what she meant were she talking philosophy, sports, or gumball machines. She cried for all the hypocrisy that existed in this imperfect world and because she had fallen victim to it. When finally she had calmed down, she became aware of a splitting headache. This was the last un-Nickie-like thing she would do, she swore, as she dialed Ruthanne's number to beg off on tonight's party. She hated to do it, but with all good will she was in no shape to celebrate.

"Of course you're coming!" Ruthanne snapped.

"I really can't. I'm sorry. My head is pounding and something happened. I'll fill you in some other time, but the way I feel, I can assure you, I'd just be a party pooper."

"Nonsense. Take two aspirins and try to rest. I'll see you at eight. Believe me, if the trouble is what I think, spelled C-R-A-I-G, it'll do you a world of good to get out."

Nickie had to laugh. "You're an incorrigible optimist. I shouldn't have taken you on. I didn't have a fighting chance."

"You'll be here then?" Ruthanne's voice was cheerful.

"See you at eight," Nickie said as she hung up.

Following her friend's advice, she swallowed the aspirin

134

and lay down. Swollen and red, her eyes hurt when she shut them as well as when she kept them open.

She was surprised to find that she was able to doze off for an hour or two. When she awoke, she was, if not refreshed, at least in possession of all her faculties. Crying jags would not get the better of her again. Moving slowly around her apartment, she put Mozart's *Eine Kleine Nachtmusik* on her stereo and drew herself a hot bath. While it was filling, she brewed a cup of Twining's orange pekoe tea and warmed up a frozen croissant, which she took with her into the bathtub. It wasn't a sybarite's champagne and caviar bathtub repast, but it did very nicely. She didn't need Craig Boone to enjoy life as long as Twining, croissants, and the makers of Joy bath oil were around!

CHAPTER ELEVEN

Ruthanne's husband pressed a punch glass into Nickie's hand. This was her fourth glass, and sweet alcoholic mixtures went directly to her head. She decided to forestall her host's further hospitality by holding that glass for the remainder of the evening.

She watched helplessly as Ruthanne's nephew, Seymour, made a beeline for her. She had spent most of the evening unsuccessfully dodging him.

"Great party, isn't it?" he boomed.

"Sure is. Ruthanne knows how to entertain."

"Yep. She puts out quite a spread, that little lady does," he said, referring to his aunt, who at five feet, eleven inches stood a half head taller than he.

"So tell me, Nickie, do you have someone managing your affairs?"

"My affairs?" Nickie laughingly thought that might be a good idea.

"You know, taking care of your finances and investing your money for you. With all of today's options, stocks, bonds, money market funds, it's a complicated business. I'm sure you don't want to fill your pretty head with the Dow Jones averages."

Seymour blinked, owllike, through his thick glasses.

With his unstylish wide lapeled jacket and white patent leather belt, Nickie thought that he was the one who could do with some management, albeit in the fashion department.

"On the contrary, I enjoy choosing my investments." Her eyes sparkled mischievously. "I'm especially interested in venture capital. I'm about to invest in an undersea exploration for sunken treasure off the coast of Mexico," she fibbed.

"You don't want to do that!" Seymour exclaimed, alarm showing plainly on his face.

"Why not? Simply because I lost everything when I put my savings behind a new pig feed is no reason to retire from the exciting world of high finance."

Seymour looked at her askance, dimly aware that he was being put on. Nickie smiled guiltily. He did, after all, mean well and he *was* her best friend's nephew.

"How did you become interested in optometry?" she queried politely.

Seymour launched into a detailed autobiographical explanation of his great fascination with the properties of glass, numbers, and all things technical. Besides, the hours were good and the money was attractive. Nickie stifled a yawn and wondered if Seymour wasn't Ruthanne's step-nephew.

"Now, Seymour," Ruthanne's voice rang out as she bustled over, "don't monopolize Nickie. Give the poor girl a chance to breathe. Circulate!"

Nickie smiled wanly at her friend.

"I suppose Seymour isn't your cup of tea," Ruthanne said, and sighed. "You do make it difficult though. There aren't a whole lot of tall, dashing athletes around."

"Ruthanne, you're too much. I promise you, I'm not in the market."

Ruthanne squeezed her arm, "I don't like to see you with such a long face. Do you want to talk about it?"

Nickie shook her head. "But thanks for the sympathy."

Ruthanne looked at her with an expression that could only be described as motherly concern. Nickie braced herself. She was sure that her friend was about to launch into one of her lessons on living, and when she and Ruthanne were converged upon by a short, plump man in a dashiki and his prim, beautifully coiffed wife, Nickie gave an audible sigh of relief.

"So this is the famous sports reporter we're always hearing about." The man held out his hand. "I'm Don Kissinger and this is my wife, Serena. We live down the street."

"Pleased to meet you," Nickie said with a smile.

The rest of the evening was passed in pleasant chatter. Everyone remarked on Ruthanne's fabulous crab canapes, indirectly compared incomes, and totally relaxed when an Atari video game miraculously appeared and competition could be channeled off in less tedious ways. Quite coordinated and something of a closet Atari buff, Nickie amazed everyone by consistently winning at Breakaway. When the party broke up around midnight, she was one of the last to leave.

"I'm glad you twisted my arm into coming. It was nice."

Ruthanne kissed the air next to Nickie's cheek and told her to drive carefully.

"I hope that wasn't a jinx," Ruthanne said of her warning when ten minutes later Nickie returned. Her car had a flat tire.

"Don't you have a spare?"

Nickie shook her head in disgust. "What used to be my spare is now my right front tire. I never got around to replacing it."

"You're not going to find an open gas station around here at this time of night, and you don't want to bother with AAA now. I'll have Bill drive you home, and you can take care of the flat tomorrow."

"My sentiments exactly."

Hearing her voice, Seymour came in from the kitchen. He put down his glass. "Trouble?"

When he heard the story he insisted that Nickie's apartment was on his way, and he wouldn't dream of letting his uncle Bill have the pleasure to himself. He would drive her.

Catching the look of dismay which flitted across Nickie's eyes, Ruthanne lifted her eyebrows, grimaced sympathetically, and whispered, "Blood may be thicker than water, but it doesn't make you blind. You sure you don't want to stay over here for the night?"

Nickie chuckled. Ruthanne was a treasure. "Thanks, but I'll sleep better in my own bed."

Seymour, his chest swelled like a rooster's, ushered her out. On the way he plied her with questions about her job. She repeatedly insisted that she could not tell him much since she was, at that moment at least, unemployed. She was as much in the dark about television reporting as he was, and radio, too closely related in her mind with Metz, was something she didn't want to think about right now. She knew that, like many men, Seymour had trouble reconciling his image of her as a lady felled by a flat tire with his image of a successful sports reporter. So to avoid what he couldn't understand he settled for talking about himself. He told her about the sign in his waiting room, "Too Little Sex Makes Your Eyes Go Bad."

"Cute, that's real cute," Nickie said dryly.

"You betcha!" he replied.

Nickie welcomed the subsequent lull in the conversation until she happened to glance over Seymour's way and noticed that his head was nodding and his eyes looked half-closed.

"Seymour!" she yelled. "Wake up!"

"What? Oh! Guess I'm a little tired. Hmm."

Nickie spent the remainder of the trip with her eyes glued to Seymour's, making sure they stayed open. She did her best to be vivacious, hoping that her simulated gaiety would be, if not infectious, at least impossible to doze by.

She breathed a sigh of relief as they pulled up in front of her apartment.

"You're coming in for a mug of black coffee," she said firmly. "Ruthanne would never forgive me if I let you drive home zonked."

Grinning at her sheepishly, Seymour followed without protest.

"You should have told me how tired you were. I would have gladly driven for you."

Nickie didn't notice, as she berated Seymour, the Maserati parked across the street with its wide-awake driver watching her and Seymour in astonishment.

She kept up a steady stream of chatter as she bustled in the kitchen washing and filling her percolator. The last thing she wanted was for him to spend the night on her sofa. Never before had she seen anybody who could fall asleep so quickly. It seemed that as soon as he had sat down in her living room his chin had fallen on his chest. It took five minutes for her to awaken him, longer by far than the time it had taken him to fall asleep. Why, oh, why, hadn't Ruthanne warned her about her nephew's quirk? This was even more ridiculous than the sign he kept in his waiting room!

Just as Nickie was bringing him a steaming mug of her strongest coffee, there sounded a rap at her door. She placed the coffee on the table in front of Seymour and went to open it. Though she didn't normally receive visitors after midnight, she opened the door.

Her gasp was audible. Craig's rugged handsomeness, a composite of longish curly hair, rugged jaw, piercing eyes, Roman nose, and a physique that would put Paul Newman to shame, had its usual effect on Nickie. She stared.

"May I come in?"

Her no came too quickly. "That is, I'm busy."

Craig nodded in the direction of the sofa. "With company?"

"You might say that."

Nickie thought she saw an amused glint in his eyes. If she were going to go for an opposite physical type to Craig, she couldn't have found a better specimen than Seymour!

"I have to talk to you about something," Craig insisted.

"It's not necessary," Nickie answered frostily. She wasn't going to let him pawn off phony excuses on her!

"You don't even know what I'm going to say," Craig exploded.

Seymour ambled over.

"You having any trouble?" He addressed Nickie.

"That's all right, Seymour. I can handle this."

Seymour retreated a step, an uncertain look on his face. Craig grabbed Nickie's arm and pulled her out into the hallway. The pressure of his fingertips on her flesh elec-

141

trified her. He pushed the door closed on Seymour's well-polished shoe.

"What's gotten into you?" His brow was furrowed in a mix of puzzlement and anger.

"Let's say I've come to my senses and leave it at that. I don't really want to talk now. . . . I don't think I want to talk to you at all, ever." She pulled back.

He tightened his grip on her arm. The nerve endings in her skin were alive with sensation, and she knew that the five red marks that he would surely leave her with were but a small sign of the force of his will.

"I would say you owe me an explanation." His voice was deadly calm.

"Do I?" She paused. "Maybe it's that I used to know exactly what was going on in my life. I don't know anything anymore." She was careful not to mention the blonde.

"That doesn't sound all that serious."

"It is to me. Now if you'll excuse me . . ."

"For God's sake, Nicole. I'm not going to beg!"

"It wouldn't help you even if you did," she tossed back. The nerve of that man! Cheating, lying, and now admitting that her feelings about her life were of no consequence.

Craig dropped her arm as if it were yesterday's newspaper. His eyes blazed with anger as he glanced from Nickie to Seymour and then back again.

"I thought we were playing on the same team. It seems I was mistaken. All right."

Nickie ached to reach out and stroke the place in his neck where his veins stood out angrily. The conflict between her desire to hold him and be held and the anger and hurt he had inflicted upon her made her doubt her sanity. How could she want to run to and away from him at the same time? He was poison to her, she knew that, and yet a source of life she had never known.

He laughed, a raw sound full of irony.

"I always believed in short romances." The corners of his wide mouth curled in disdain.

"You'd better go now," Nickie whispered. She didn't trust herself to speak aloud.

Craig sneered derisively. "I will. But first one for the road." He caught her up in both his arms. They felt like steel vises around her. His stare was threatening, his lips which fastened on her mouth bruising. He took her slightly parted lips as if they belonged to him.

"Craig, no," she gasped. "You said you'd go. Don't do this!"

"Your body speaks a language of its own," he answered huskily. She knew he was referring to the taut nipples that responded instantly to the sweeping caress of his hands and to her mouth, which answered his kisses even as she fought him. She knew now as she had known before that giving herself to him was too dangerous. It would mean the loss of herself. There was too much mystery to him, too much power, too much passion. It was a passion, she suspected, not only reserved for her, but for everything and everyone he approached. And like all those other people and things, like the fans or the ball fitted snugly in his glove, she was in his control. She would not tolerate it! With all her strength she pushed him back. He looked down speculatively at her white face.

"Why," he queried mockingly, "is it that
a woman what she really wants she gives
for it?"

143

"You give me what *you* really want!" she retaliated scathingly.

"You try a man's patience, Nicole. I don't understand it but I've had it!"

As if he had caught a belated cue, Seymour stepped out into the corridor. He stood with his legs planted apart, his arms folded over his concave chest and a grim scowl on his face.

"You had better get a move on. It sounds like the lady wants you gone."

As he got the words out of his mouth, Seymour moved in front of Nickie ready to fend off any blows. Craig's eyes swept over Seymour quickly and what she saw welling up in them could be nothing but amusement. She had to admit that the sight of Seymour ready to take on "the great Craig Boone," who could surely make pudding out of him with one blow, was indeed absurd.

"Are you threatening me with the use of force, sir?" Craig asked.

Nickie could tell that it was with an effort that he kept a straight face. A little comic relief never hurt, she thought mournfully.

"Well," Seymour hedged. He stuck out his chin resolutely. "I'll do what I have to do . . ."

"To protect the lady's honor," Craig finished the sentence for him. Mirth bubbled up in his eyes, threatening to spill over, she feared, in gales of laughter. She felt like decking him. "No need, I was on my way anyhow," he assured him magnanimously. "She's a wild one. Perhaps you can tame her." His countenance was conspiratorial, and he winked broadly at Seymour.

Seymour's chest puffed out visibly. If she hadn't been wary of hurting Seymour's feelings, she would have indig-

144

nantly pointed out that this was no time for jokes. It served, however, to strengthen her resolve. He could never take her seriously, not even now.

Seymour stood aside and with a gallant flourish bade her enter her own apartment. He resumed his former position on her sofa, only now he placed his arm along its upholstered back while he looked at her expectantly. Clearly he was waiting for some sort of grateful recompense for services almost rendered.

"Did you finish your coffee, Seymour?" she asked as she looked at his empty mug. "Need a refill?"

"I'm okay. Why don't you have a seat?" He patted the sofa.

"It's late. Why don't we call it a night?" Nickie put on her most charming smile. "I have a lot to do tomorrow to prepare for Monday."

"Sure. Well, I guess I'd better get going. Uh, can I call you sometime?"

"Of course. I'll be swamped for the next few weeks though. Thanks a lot for driving me home and," she added, "for everything." It was worth the white lie. He probably thought he was a great hero.

It seemed like hours by the time he finally shuffled out the door. It couldn't have been more than ten minutes, but Nickie was beginning to feel as if her world was caving in. Had she really said those things to Craig? Was it really over? It had to be. She was just one of his women, nothing more and nothing less. What she did have was the distinction of being a sports personality in her own right. Winding up as a Boone groupie was not what she had envisaged for her life! She thought of the way it felt when he made love to her. She shut it out. She would find someone else. There were plenty of men around.

Winding her hair around her fingers, she squeezed her eyes shut. How had she ever gotten into this mess? Unbidden, a picture of Craig with his arm about that woman sprang to her mind. Her instincts after she had gotten home and over the first shock of betrayal were to confront him, to yell and scream and shake her fists. The intensity of her jealousy stunned her, for it seemed at times to consume her. She thought that if she let herself she could act exactly like a fishwife. She was grateful for her strong sense of decorum.

Though she could have spent the night pacing, she forced herself to go to bed. She plumped up her pillow, snuggled between cool Marimekko sheets, and stared with eyes that refused to close at the starless sky.

Sleep was fitful, her dreams disturbing. She awoke early and spent the morning refusing to admit to herself that she was waiting for the phone to ring. There was no welcome jangle to jar her out of her self-imposed stupor, not even a wrong number.

It was noon before she decided to get on with it. She phoned the station's hairdresser, who promised to be over that afternoon. Free hairdressers were one of the perquisites of television jobs. She would be cooperative, she decided, let the man do whatever he wanted with her long locks as long as he didn't cut more than half an inch! But before he came, she had better get her car from Ruthanne's street. She dialed a local cab company to come and pick her up right away. She needed to be driven to a gas station, where she would purchase a tire, and then on to Ruthanne's. Last year, tired of not knowing a muffler from a carburetor, Nickie had taken a "powder puff" auto mechanics course at a local adult school. Other than filling her own gas tank and checking the oil at self-service sta-

146

tions, she had not had the opportunity to call on her newly acquired skills. This would be the test.

The driver, a grizzled wizened man of indeterminate age, recognized her voice and correctly guessed her identity. He asked for her autograph, a first in Nickie's experience, and offered to change the tire for her. Nickie thanked him but assured him, as she paid her fare and added a generous tip, that she could handle it.

Standing at her car, the jack and tire upright beside her, she decided she would knock on Ruthanne's door only after the fact. She didn't need an audience for this maiden voyage into the world of the do-it-yourselfers. She had taken notes from the course along and knew, as she consulted them for the first steps, that she must look ridiculous to any unseen onlookers. It took her more than an hour, but finally, full of grease and sweat, she stood up to admire the new tire. Now she could drive across the Sahara if she wanted to! She smiled in triumph, having forgotten for a while how blue she felt. Little successes could always do that for her, she mused.

Ruthanne, when she heard, was impressed.

"I'd offer you a toast, but I think you'd prefer a hot shower," she grinned, wrinkling her nose.

Nickie laughed. "I'm on my way. I only wanted to demonstrate that I'm a woman of many trades."

"I knew that. By the way, my poor nephew is hopelessly smitten. He wouldn't get off the phone last night, just kept going on and on about you. What did you do, bewitch him?"

"Oh, Ruthanne!"

"Don't worry. He'll get over it. Anything new on the Craig front?"

"You make it sound like I'm fighting a war." She

cocked her head. "Maybe I am, in a way. But it's the two sides of myself that are doing battle. And it's the rational me that's winning!"

"You don't sound too happy about it."

Nickie's eyebrows shot up. "But I am. Of course I am."

"Should it be such a battle?" Ruthanne looked at her quizzically.

"Craig's not right for me. Our life-styles wouldn't gel. I don't even know how seriously he took the whole thing. It was a lark for him. But that's all right. We had some good times. I have some nice memories. That's all you can really hope for. Nothing lasts. Even when people don't separate physically, the ones who are the most apart, the ones you see in restaurants without anything to say to one another, those are the married ones. It's better this way."

"If you keep saying those words to yourself, maybe you'll end up by believing them," Ruthanne said dryly.

Nickie tore her eyes from her friend's face and looked around nervously.

"I don't know how you manage to keep this place so tidy and homey what with a full-time job and a family."

"Now, honey, you don't really want to talk about housework, do you?"

"Give me a break, Ruthanne. I don't know my own mind. How can I know what I want to say?" She shook her head slowly. "Should I say I love him?" Maybe I do. But it's not going to change anything. He's got other women coming out of the woodwork. I saw him with someone, all lovey-dovey, just yesterday out at the airport. I don't need that aggravation."

"Perhaps you should talk to him about it, bend a little."

"Far enough to snap? No thanks."

"Aren't you *ever* going to see him again?"

"I don't know," Nickie responded wearily. "We kind of have a date to see the Japanese baseball exhibit, but I doubt if he'll call now, and even if he does, I'm not going to let myself be taken in by him again."

Ruthanne sighed. "You start your new job tomorrow. Nervous?"

"A little. I hope there are no Stan Metzes there. And I hope I film well."

"Didn't they do a screen test?" Ruthanne asked, surprised.

"No, the producer mentioned it, but I gave him an audition tape I'd made at WRPJ and then he said"— Nickie laughed self-consciously—"that with my bones there should be no problem."

"Well, he's right," Ruthanne said confidently. "You've got it all."

"Don't I though?" Nickie retorted glumly.

In the rush of learning all there was to know in her job Nickie was rarely at home those first days. When she was at her apartment, she often found herself too tired to think. It was a respite she welcomed from thoughts of Craig which made her despondent.

When the phone rang one evening, she answered it automatically, forgetting to wonder, as she was wont to do, if it was he.

"Hello."

"Hi," Craig's voice was subdued.

"Hi," Nickie echoed warily.

"How's the job?"

"Oh, fine thanks."

"So, it's working out for you?"

"Yeh—hectic."

"Uh, well, about that exhibit on Japanese baseball history, I think I'll be tied up."

"I can imagine," she said with a sniff.

"You're good at imagining things, aren't you?" He paused. "So was my ex-wife. I never liked being grilled and doubted. Anyway this isn't why I called. There's something I want to talk to you about."

"There's nothing to talk about," Nickie retorted.

There was a long silence before Craig finally answered, his voice so low and husky she could barely hear him. "Maybe you're right after all."

The telephone clicked in Nickie's ear. For the seconds she stood there, Nickie was unable to tell whether the buzz which replaced the angry silence was in her head or in the receiver.

She tried without success to resume her mindless state. All she could think about was his call. What was he going to tell her? Was he finally going to play it straight with her? She would never know now. It was too late.

CHAPTER TWELVE

Monday, a week later, Nickie looked at her watch. It was twelve o'clock and time to meet Ruthanne for lunch. She closed her notebook, locked her desk, and hurried out to the elevator. She was to meet her friend at a crêperie that was located halfway between their respective studios. Since she had refused at least half a dozen dates with Seymour in the past week, she was slightly apprehensive about this luncheon with his aunt.

Just as she pressed the down button, a jean-clad assistant accosted her with the news that she would be responsible for the commentary on this evening's game since Mort Cunningham, the station's regular commentator, had called in to say he was incapacitated by a bout of intestinal flu.

"Righto!" Nickie answered, a blasé look on her face. Inwardly, she was exhilarated. She felt like jumping and cheering. Her first time doing a play-by-play on television! This would be the first time in the history of Seattle television that a woman had been so privileged.

"What a coup! Congratulations!" Ruthanne exclaimed when she heard.

"I hope I can pull it off," Nickie said doubtfully. "I've

never done an entire game live except"—she laughed—"simulated in front of my mirror at home."

"That's called pregame jitters. You'll do just fine. I know you."

"Guess I'll have to rise to the occasion. It's weird. You look forward to something for so long, and then the opportunity comes and you feel like you'd rather mop your floors than grab it."

"That's human nature. If you never do anything, then you can't mess it up. So how's the job? What are the people like?"

"The job's wonderful. I have a lot more leeway than at WRPJ, and the people are super. Oh, once or twice I was a little irritated when people identified me as Boone's woman, as if the only reason I had gotten the job was through connections. But after they saw me at work, their attitudes changed. They really like me there, Ruthanne."

"As well they should." Ruthanne reached across the table to pat her hand. "Stan Metzes are fortunately a rare breed. By the way, you'll be interested to know that our high-and-mighty manager has been demoted. Stan is now assistant manager. Can you guess the reason why?" Ruthanne grinned conspiratorially.

"He spent too much time running in Mr. Affability contests?" Nickie ventured.

"You're close. Actually he was blamed for a point and a half fall in our ratings last week. They said it was due to his poor judgment—get ready for this—in firing you!"

Nickie opened her eyes wide. "How come revenge is so sweet?"

"No one can say he didn't deserve it. Your highly touted replacement is like every other Joe Jocularity that you hear on every other radio station. And I for one will never forgive Metz. There's simply no one for me to exchange knowing looks with anymore."

"I wish we were working together too. Maybe in our next jobs!"

"Or our next lives," Ruthanne added glumly. "Anything new with Craig?"

"No, that's over. *Finita la commedia.* I'm so busy learning the ropes at Channel seven that I don't have much time to think about a social life."

"Nickie!" Ruthanne's voice was reproachful. "Look who you're talking to. You don't have to pretend with me."

Nickie's pursed lips relaxed into a careless grimace.

"I haven't heard from him. It's for the best."

"That's a bitter medicine you've prescribed for yourself."

Her head tilted to the side, Nickie held up her palms in a gesture of resignation.

Ruthanne spent the remainder of the luncheon filling Nickie's head with well-meant advice. She told her, as if Nickie never herself opened a newspaper, how to dress for success and what movies she must not miss. She told her how to avoid breaking any more hearts, as Nickie had Seymour's.

When Nickie got back to the station, she was glad, as much as she adored Ruthanne, that no one here felt comfortable enough around her to give her lessons on living.

With Mort Cunningham at home sick, Nickie had no one to brief her on the technicalities of a live TV commentary. It was a kind of Catch-22, for had Mort been around to help her she wouldn't have been doing the game. She decided to trust her better judgment, her talent, and the crew, who would hopefully let her know which camera to look at.

With so much hustle, bustle, and excitement before each game you would think that the crew itself was going to be playing. Nickie was surprisingly calm before her big debut and in order to keep it that way decided to drive herself to the game.

Though she arrived at King Dome Stadium an hour before game time, she noted the few diehard fans who were already in the stands. She stifled a longing which overcame her to stand on the pitcher's mound as Craig would do tonight. To stand on that mound of dirt, isolated, bathed by floodlights in the night, with thousands of eyes from the packed tiers of seats concentrating on your slightest flinch—that had to be heaven.

She wondered how it would be, reporting on Craig's performance tonight as if he meant nothing more to her than he did to any other announcer who wanted the home team to win. Luckily, she had little time for such ruminations. The crew arrived, the stadium filled up, and Nickie could see the manager giving a last-minute briefing to the team. The pregame interviews and small talk, which she had done so many times before, helped Nickie to reestablish her self-confidence. She had to have it in her to do a decent play-by-play! For years she had been gearing up for this moment. She prayed that the words would roll off her tongue with professional glibness.

Game time. Nickie's heart was racing. *Here goes,* she thought. *I'll be made now or broken.* With her first call, her voice, which had started out quavery, grew in strength and clarity.

"Bobby Britton's the lead-off hitter for the Cleveland Indians. Bobby's having himself a good year after an op-

154

eration on his knee during the off season. He's hitting .301 and the fleet centerfielder has been the backbone of the Indians' outfield this year.

"Boone looks down for the sign and the first pitch, a fast ball high and inside. Ball one . . ."

Nickie glanced quickly at the crew surrounding her. Thinking that they all looked infinitely more relaxed than they had five minutes ago, she realized that they had been as nervous as she about her performance. And they were unaware that she hadn't been altogether certain that she would be able to utter Boone's name without croaking.

Catching her eye, the audio man whispered, "You're doing fine. Keep it up."

Nickie winked at him. That was the last, until the game ended, that she was conscious of a world outside the diamond. Only Craig had the power to distract her, and with an iron-clad will she forced herself to concentrate on his pitches rather than his body. She became, she felt, a part of the game, calling plays almost as they were executed.

"Jerry Granville's up now. He's two for three tonight. Line drive single to left, a pop fly to second base, and a double off the wall in the sixth inning. Boone's been having trouble with him all night.

"Two outs, runners on second and third. If Boone can wiggle himself out of this jam, he'll be lucky. Boone checks the runners, looks down for the sign, fires a popup. High infield popup! Matthews calls for it. Third base line and Boone and the Vikings are out of a tight situation! Going into the bottom of the sixth inning, Boone and the Vikings hold on to a precarious three-to-two lead."

Nickie kept up the pace and quality of her call so that when the game ended with a four-to-three victory for the Vikings, she felt like collapsing, as if she had run the bases and chased the fly balls herself. Smiling gratefully at all the well-wishers who surrounded her, she agreed that she had crossed a milestone tonight both for herself and for Seattle's women in sports. Considering her success she thought it somehow not seemly that she looked forward so impatiently to the start of the basketball season when Craig Boone would not have to be the focus of her professional scrutiny.

Praise was heaped upon her back at the studio as well. For a first play-by-play Nickie's commentary was extraordinary, they said. Her knowledgeability and the smoothness of her delivery did them all proud. Through it all Nickie glowed. How different this reception from the one she had come to expect at WRPJ.

A pall blanketed her when she agreed to view herself and the game at a studio playback. She also happened to catch some past game clips which had not been aired. There was Craig, surrounded by well-wishers, too many of them pretty girls who were probably not, Nickie guessed, overly interested in baseball. With bitterness Nickie thought that it hadn't taken him long to replace her. But what could she have expected? His second job seemed to be making women fall in love with him. At least she could be thankful that she had restrained herself on the occasions when she had almost dialed Craig's number. Even those moments when she envisioned a future filled with Seymours—or even worse.

Realistically her social life had never needed a boost, but she told herself, even Nickie Alexander was allowed occasional bouts of insecurity. And she could allow herself occasional silliness for she knew that the last reason she would ever pursue a man, especially Craig, was desperation.

Two weeks later, Mort Cunningham was called out of town, and Nickie was once again thrust in the position of play-by-play commentator. She exceeded her own expectations that time. When he returned Mort spoke to her with mock gravity, claiming that she was too good and might steal his job.

"That would never happen, Mort. You're tops. And I would never attempt it. When you get to know me better, you'll find that I don't play dirty."

Continuing in the innovative tradition she had begun to develop back at the radio station, she started a fan-of-the-week interview on her segment. She interviewed a man in his sixties who hadn't missed a home game since the Vikings had come to Seattle, and a hotdog vendor who had come from Greece five years ago and who had embraced his new country by becoming a baseball fanatic. She interviewed a young boy she had noticed sitting in the dugout who was assistant to the ball boys.

"What's your name, kid?" She held out the mike to him.

"Joey."

"Hi, Joey. I've seen you sitting out here in the dugout. How did you manage it?"

"I help the ball boys sometimes. My friend got me the job."

"Ah-hah! Who's your friend?"

"The best pitcher in the world, Craig Boone. I'm gonna grow up and be a pitcher just like him."

I wouldn't wish that on you, Nickie thought. The way her heart raced each time she caught a glimpse of him or heard his name depressed her.

"What do you do besides helping the ball boys and going to the games? Do you go to school?"

"Sure. Everyone goes to school." He looked at Nickie

as if she were a moron. She felt like one. She did a lot better interviewing adults, she rationalized.

"I collect baseball cards too," Joey added proudly. "I have all the Brooklyn Dodgers cards from the 1950s."

"That must be worth a lot of money."

"Yep. When I grow up, I'm gonna have the world's best collection of cards."

"And no doubt you'll also be the Vikings' lead pitcher," Nickie commented with a smile to the camera that said kids were cute and wouldn't it be a nice world if it all came out the way they planned at the age of ten.

"That's what I said," Joey grinned jauntily.

"It's been nice talking with you, Joey, and I know our viewers join me in wishing you the best of luck and a 1963 Pete Rose vintage-year card."

A program she did on futuristic baseball equipment turned out to be more controversial than she would have predicted. People, it seemed, did not want see through catchers' mitts or electric computers on gloves to eliminate hand signals. Gizmos such as audio receivers on managers', coaches', and hitters' hats were perceived by many as a threat to the American Way.

With it all the station's ratings climbed, and Nickie soon became the darling of TV sports. The pain in her heart had dulled only slightly, and though she told herself she had everything in the world to be happy about, she occasionally found herself crying for no reason. It was with some relief that toward the end of the baseball season she went to cover the first basketball game.

158

CHAPTER THIRTEEN

The same light rain that had accompanied Nickie the last time she walked along the waterfront that magic afternoon with Craig, saturated the air now. Gray fog swirled around her, enveloped her. She didn't know exactly why she had come here. She had told herself that a walk would do her good and that she needed the exercise. She had been working hard lately, and the basketball game she had just covered was nearby. What better place to unwind than by the water? She had to admit to herself, as bits and pieces of that long and irrevocably past afternoon floated into her consciousness, that she was doing precious little unwinding.

She thought of going into the ice cream place where that jolly man had given her and Craig the amaretto ice cream. In a self-punishing mood she followed her impulse. The ice cream parlor looked the same; there was still the brass railing and Tiffany lamps. The proprietor looked the same; he still had his handlebar mustache and paunch. What was painfully different was his reaction to her. He barely looked at her as he handed her a cone and change. He had been so friendly the last time. Craig had said that the world was in love with love. Clichés were often true. She and Craig must have looked like lovers, reminding all who crossed their path of the beauty of romance. Alone she didn't exist for this ice cream man. Sometimes she didn't know if she existed for herself. She didn't really want to eat the ice cream and threw it into the nearest trash can.

As she walked in and out of curio shops, nothing much held her interest. Her feet led her to the pier, a solitary presence, her hands deep in her pockets and her collar turned up. She felt as if she had just stepped out of a Sherlock Holmes movie, the tragic, haunted heroine. She almost laughed out loud at her fantasy. What a romantic bent of mind she kept concealed under her veneer of rationalism! Given half a chance, who knows, she might prefer Blake or Du Maurier to *Sports Illustrated*!

Of course, you didn't survive in the fiercely competitive world of sports reporting by spending your time reading poems. She almost expressed her feelings with her hands. She caught herself in time lest the few passersby back at the shops think she was some kind of strange bird. Since it had ended with Craig, she had found herself, from time to time, talking out loud as if he were standing next to her. She told herself over and over that it was better now that he was gone, that she was freer. Yet still, she thought of many things she would like to tell him, that only he would understand.

Standing by the pier, she could barely see its tip, so thick and low was the fog. The rhythmic lapping of the sea against the mossy stones in front left her with a feeling of timelessness. The acrid smell of empty lobster traps piled like so many chicken coops induced her to dare the slippery walk out on the weather-worn pier. She could have been walking a pirate's plank, but for the warm breeze that soothed and the solitude that surrounded her. She wished she could shake the familiar feeling of dread that accom-

160

panied her of late, when she wasn't occupied with the business of living. It was so beautiful here that she should have been filled with nothing but sea sounds, salt air, and calm.

"Hello."

Her mind was playing tricks on her, Nickie thought, as she stared persistently out into the pea-soup fog. She was hearing things now. Maybe she needed a vacation.

"Did you miss me?"

Nickie spun around. "Craig!" Her eyes opened wide. "What are you doing here?"

"Following a hunch. Good old-fashioned telepathy, based on the knowledge that the basketball game is nearby, and you were nowhere else to be found. Did you miss me?" he repeated.

Though his tone was neutral, almost flip, Nickie didn't miss the warm expression in his eyes. She had never known anyone whose eyes could speak so eloquently, so clearly.

"Yes . . . I did." Hope she had assumed dead was ignited with a flare.

"It's been hell without you, Nicole," he answered gruffly. "If there's one thing I detest, it's an indispensable woman."

"You've always known how to give a compliment." It was easy, this banter. Would she be able, she wondered, to talk about real things? There were things that had to be said. After seeing him again she still wanted him—all of him. Was that the problem?

"What do you say to an Irish coffee?"

"Just like old times, huh?"

"With some minor corrections, I hope."

161

He took her arm. It felt like yesterday that they had been walking like this. It was almost six weeks.

"Are we going to the same café? The one with the brick fireplace?"

"No. There's a tavern across the street that looks out on the water. How have you been?"

"I can't complain. My job is great. What about you?"

"I've been hanging in there. Had my ups and downs. I've thought about you a lot."

"Have you? What took you so long to seek me out?"

"Two can seek as well as one. Listen, I don't like games, except . . . sometimes when a terrible thing happens you see the world differently. You know what matters. I guess we both needed a cooling-off period."

"What are you talking about, Craig?" Nickie's eyebrows were knit. "What terrible thing happened? You're not ill, are you?"

"No, not me. Wait till we sit down."

They walked the rest of the way to the tavern in silence. It felt good to be next to him, like being home again. They sat at a corner table next to a bay window. Craig ordered the drinks.

"Wonderful view of the fog from here," Nickie observed.

She leaned further across the table than was necessary for so casual a comment, as if she were saying something important. Breathing deeply she caught a whiff of his musky aftershave. It was a reassuringly masculine scent, one which she always identified with him. Craig sprawled casually in the wide wooden chair, studying her with a half smile.

"You look good. Suffering agrees with you, if suffering is what you've been doing."

162

"There are degrees of suffering," she said quietly. "I won't pretend it compares to torture on a rack. Anyway I never used the word suffering. I admitted that I missed you. But I go along, rather well in fact." She jutted out her chin, not sure how to take his kidding. "You don't look bad yourself," she fibbed.

Actually he looked awful. He had dark rings under his eyes and a haggard look she had never seen on him before. She wondered for a thrilling moment if it was because of her.

"Come on," he chuckled. "How can I believe anything you say?"

"I tell the truth when it's important," she defended herself. "Well, what is it? Haven't you been sleeping enough?"

Craig grimaced. He made a fist with one hand which he pounded into his other. The pain she had seen in his eyes out on the pier returned.

"I had a friend once. We grew up together." His voice cracked. "Louise was more than a friend, an older sister, really." He swallowed. "She passed away last week. She saw it happening. It was a long futile year she spent going from doctor to doctor. There was nothing anyone could do."

"I'm sorry."

As if he didn't hear or as if condolences were too trivial to acknowledge, he droned on: "She left a little boy. Joey is ten years old and he's all alone, except for me. Louise made the requisite legal arrangements, so he'll be in my charge now. I'm going to do my damndest to make up to that kid for all he's suffered."

Nickie's face, betraying her pity for Joey and her empathy, looked pinched and momentarily older. She saw herself, nineteen years ago. With a start, she remembered the cute little boy she had interviewed in the dugout. Joey was his name.

"The last month or two have been the worst. Why, it's odd. The last time I saw Louise in any kind of shape was the final weekend you and I spent together. You made that big fuss about skydiving. You didn't know, how could you have, that all I was doing was helping a dying lady live her last wish. She figured she was fading anyway, so it wouldn't make much of a difference if she went while jumping. At least she'd have a thrill and the kid might have been able to collect double indemnity on the insurance. There was no way anything could have actually happened during the jump anyway. There's the safety chute in case the primary parachute doesn't open. The worst she could have done was sprain an ankle."

Nickie looked at him wide-eyed. Her heart was pounding.

"You mean that was Louise?" she stammered.

Craig looked at her strangely. "What *are* you talking about?" A light seemed to go on in his eyes. "You saw us? Ah-hah. That explains some things."

Nickie looked down at her mug of Irish coffee. She took a big sip of the hot beverage, grateful that the bartender had been heavy-handed with the whiskey.

"So that's what it was all about," he continued. "If it wasn't so tragic it would be funny."

Nickie felt a blush creeping up past her ears. She wished she were playing this scene in black and white.

"That was a minor issue," she replied offhandedly. "I'm not afraid of competition."

"Didn't you just say a moment ago that when it was

important you told the truth? You don't have to save face. We're not Samurai warriors."

She put her chin in her hands. "All right. If I'm to be involved with someone, it's going to be on somewhat of an exclusive basis. You've got too many women."

"Now that at least sounds like an honest sentiment. Absurd, but honest. In any case, to set the record straight, there are no other women in my life, at least none of any consequence. There was Louise. In some ways our relationship was deeper than many a marriage, but it wasn't romantic." A faraway look came into his eyes. "God, I'll miss her! She didn't have an easy life."

Nickie reached out to lay a hand on his arm. "I'm so sorry."

Even with his haggardness or perhaps because of it Craig looked beautiful to her. His was an inner as well as an outer beauty.

"Is there a husband?"

"Her husband ran away when she was pregnant with Joey. He never saw the kid. Her parents were stiff-necked, unbending, punishing people. They disowned her when she started going around with the guy. Said he was a good-for-nothing. It turns out they were right, but it also turns out that they weren't such prizes themselves. I can never understand people who will turn away their own flesh and blood, and pretend they're doing it for a greater good." Craig's voice was hard.

"She was lucky to have found such a good friend," Nickie said gently.

"I did what I could, but she wouldn't take much. During the off season I'd spend Saturdays with Joey but in season it's rough. I'd wind up squeezing him in somewhere. I've been bringing him along to games recently—letting him sit in the dugout and help the ball boys."

Nickie closed her eyes. So that was it!

"Is that where you were the night of Ruthanne's party?"

"That's right." Craig hesitated. "You didn't think . . . ? Oh, no!"

They stared at each other. "I'm sorry," they blurted out in unison.

"I shouldn't have been so secretive. I didn't want to talk about Louise. I suppose I was afraid all along you wouldn't really understand, that you'd be hurt and suspicious. Maybe even say you wanted to see other men. I told myself that I didn't have to explain my actions to you. You know, my old hang-up about not having to be accountable to *any* woman." He paused and looked down at his hands. "I can see now how wrong that was; how foolish it was of me not to come to you, to trust that you would understand."

Nickie's heart went out to him. She covered his hand with her own, certain that she would always find forgiveness in her heart for him.

"I shouldn't have been so suspicious. It was my fault," Nickie countered.

He was right, she mused. He was secretive. What was odd about Craig was that he gave the impression of openness. You felt that he was all up front. She was just learning that he only showed what he cared to share. She thought of his personality as multilayered, like the strata of rock she had admired when they were cross-country skiing. As she had examined each layer, she had thought that it was so hard and well formed that there was nothing else underneath except maybe molten lava at its core. But she knew of course that if it was somehow peeled away, there would be a still deeper layer.

Nickie suddenly recalled the picture she had once seen in a newspaper of Craig with a woman and child. That must have been Louise and Joey.

Craig drained the dregs of his Irish coffee and ordered another.

"So how's work? I saw you on the tube a few times. You were super. I was proud."

"It's marvelous, Craig. The people are friendly, and I get to moderate the games sometimes, do interviews, the works. I have the kind of freedom I never had at WRPJ. The money's not bad either."

"So you think you might resist an offer from the *Today* show?"

"I wouldn't go that far. But it suits me fine for the time being."

"A couple of people came up to talk to me," Craig announced suddenly. "One from the Atlanta organization and one from Philly. I could be a free agent next season."

Nickie felt her spirits plummet.

"Anything tangible?" She didn't want to hear the answer.

"Yep. Atlanta's offering me a good deal more money, a nice rotation, some sweeteners."

"Are you going to take it?" Nickie knew her voice sounded breathless.

"I don't know. Probably not."

"How come?"

"I like Seattle, I like this team. Where else can you go cross-country skiing in the summer?"

"Alaska."

"Yes, well, you got me thinking about that igloo, and

I thought better of it too," he said, and chuckled. "You know, I'm not going to be playing much longer. I'm no youngster. At thirty-two I figure I've got another two, three good pitching years ahead of me. And my company's here. So's my future."

Her relief that he was staying put was tempered by the realization that *her* future depended heavily on moving about. Newscasters and sportscasters were notorious job-hoppers. It was the only way to get ahead. If you were stuck in a market like Beaumont, Texas, which rated one hundred twentieth, you would do anything to move to Indianapolis, which was the twenty-first biggest. And if you were in Indianapolis and got an offer from Phila-delphia, the fourth market, or the Big Apple, number one, you'd have to be a fool not to move. Maybe down the road she'd have the opportunity to cover the World Series. Nothing would keep her away. So why her relief at Craig's decision to stay? Any way you sliced it, their liaison had to be temporary.

As if he were guessing her thoughts, Craig modified his remarks. "Moving's okay for some people. But a two-year stint somewhere doesn't thrill me. You finished with your coffee? I feel like walking."

Nickie appreciated what she perceived as an attempt at diplomacy, but it didn't change anything. In her profes-sion two-year stints were about average. If the ratings went up a point, you got to stay on and got a fat salary increase. You could also get recruited by the bigger mar-kets. If the ratings went down a point, you were out on your ear. She knew it didn't sound like much to most people, but a point fluctuation in the ratings could mean millions of dollars in lost or gained revenues to the televi-sion stations. It was a tough business she had chosen.

Once outside, Nickie blinked. The fog had lifted and the sun was shining like a beacon through the clouds. Craig's hand had found hers and their fingers intertwined. Her hand, though of average size, felt lost in his. Thousands of balls spinning at enormous speeds from his fingertips had left them hardened and smooth, almost as if they were sheathed in steel.

"Hey, Boone! Way to go! Keep it up!" a young dock-worker greeted him.

Craig smiled and waved.

"Give them five more years, and they won't recognize me even if they're sharing the same elevator. The public's got a short memory," he muttered.

"Does that bother you?"

"Not at all. What about you?"

"I plan to stay in the public eye permanently."

"To each his own poison," he said with a chuckle. "I like your confidence. It's very attractive."

It might be attractive, she thought darkly, but it was also the major obstacle to any future with Craig. She didn't want to lose him again; she couldn't give up her career. If it wasn't jealousy and bitter suspicion that would separate them, it was ambition and distance. She supposed she simply wasn't one of those people destined for the whole pie. She would have to settle for a slice. Somehow she knew she would not be able to make that decision. She would not say to Craig that she was choosing a career over him. Yet she would never quit her job. How could she? Too much of her life had been geared toward this career of hers to throw it away. But when she was with Craig, she was a fuller, happier Nickie Alexander. Why did life have to be so complicated, she anguished.

"Baseball has been good to me," he continued. "But

169

when it's time, I'll know and get out. Lately, not only the business, but also the technology of my software company has been interesting me more and more. It'll be good to devote more time to it. And then," his voice softened, "I'm going to need more time at home for Joey. He's going to need a lot of care. It wouldn't hurt for him to have a stepmother either." The last was uttered so casually that Nickie barely had time to react.

"Having lost my only role model at too tender an age, I wouldn't have the slightest idea of how to go about it. I wouldn't know how to react to being called 'mother.' "

Nickie's hands felt clammy. She hoped she hadn't been presumptuous in answering thus.

"We could call you Uncle Nickie," Craig teased. "Hey, look at that fishing boat coming in. It's really riding low in the water."

Nickie smiled thinly, not sure of her ground. Glancing at the trawler piled high with fish, she thought of the freckle-faced, towheaded little boy she had seen in the dugout, and her heart went out to him. This was no joking matter, this question of stepparentage. Then she imagined what a child born of Craig and herself would look like.

Marriage was not a joking matter either, but Craig had never broached the subject in any other way. She must learn to adjust, to stop taking everything he said to heart. Goodness knows, she was able to do that with other people. That was one reason she had gotten so far. She had an uncanny ability to know when someone was faking or covering up. She called it her instant bullshit detector. It had made her respected for her sports interviews, for she always knew the right question to ask, when to pull back, or when to go in for the kill. She had had athletes admitting things to her on the air that they wouldn't have told their own mothers. There was the time Al Dawson had confessed to using his college coach's credit cards for fancy dinners and fancy women, the time Ira Marks had told her he was shot up full of pain-killing drugs before each game, and the time Gordon Martins had confessed that he didn't possess much team spirit and that he played only for the greater glory of Gordon Martins. The only time her I.B.S.D. didn't work was with Craig. She was absolutely unable to psych him out. Maybe, she mused, that was part of his fascination.

"How's your friend?" he asked, "the one who so gallantly came to your rescue by kicking me out?"

"Oh, that's Seymour," Nickie said, and laughed self-consciously. "Ruthanne's nephew."

Craig chuckled. "Has he been taking good care of you in my absence?"

"I haven't seen him since. He was good enough to drive me home, that's all. You've been knocking around with various women though."

"Not true. I've had a hard time shaking some groupies without getting mauled, if that's what you're referring to."

"How's Jo-Jo?" Nickie asked hastily.

"He's asked about you once or twice. He never did that with anyone else I've taken out. It looks like you made a hit."

"Jo-Jo has good taste," Nickie teased, "and he makes the world's best chicken soup."

Craig led her back on the pier. Whereas the fog had almost hidden it from view a short while ago, the bright sunlight which had emerged allowed her to see it clearly now. The gray rickety slats, the seaweed, and green slime underfoot, seemed to bounce off the sun's rays. She looked up at Craig's face. Like the pier, it changed with the light.

By candlelight his complexion had a translucent quality, rare among men. Now it looked swarthy, as if he had been voyaging on rough seas. His eyes were narrow slits.

Letting go her hand, he stopped in his tracks. Without a word, with only the light from the sea reflected in his eyes, he slid his fingers through the blue-black locks of her hair, lifting and dropping the shimmering strands. She looked up at him with parted lips, waiting for his kiss. To taste him, to feel him, she hadn't known how great her desire. Had he given her half a chance she would have gladly rolled with him in the mud beneath the pier. But as abruptly as he had held her by her hair and by his gaze, he let her go. He walked on as if nothing had transpired.

Nickie feared she would trip, for her knees felt like jelly, or more appropriately, she thought, as if they had no more substance than that of the grayish pink jellyfish she occasionally sidestepped. The more things change, the more they remain the same. She thought of the maxim. The time that had passed without seeing him meant nothing. Had she been eighty-five and had he grabbed her by silvery locks she was certain that arthritic knees would turn to the same brand of jelly. This man had power!

Neither interrupting his stride nor looking at her, Craig spoke: "I usually don't believe in second chances, never in third. I hope you know your mind, Nicole."

Nickie looked down at her feet. What could she say? Whither thou goest shall I follow? That would be a blatant lie. But she could no more tell him the naked truth. To tell him that she was unalterably committed to her career, that she shied from the way he made her feel vulnerable and weak as much as she yearned for it would be disastrous. He would be perfectly justified in telling *her* to take a long walk on a short pier.

"Craig, I . . ."

"Don't say anything now. There's time."

"Craig," she said, and moistened her lips. "Why didn't you ever mention Louise or Joey? I know it was painful, but I thought we were close enough to each other."

"I don't know."

"You don't like to talk about your past, do you? Or about things that touch you? I don't know very much about your family or your childhood or even about your friends."

"I was hatched. I'll take you to meet the mother hen. She's down in Sacramento. She'll like you." He grinned. "She likes anyone who likes me."

"Would that be my only redeeming quality?"

"Your only necessary quality. By the way, are you going to be at tomorrow's game?"

"Do you think anything could keep me away from the last game of the season? I'll be sharing coverage with Mort Cunningham, the sports anchor for the show. Are you planning on pitching another perfect game?" she said flirtatiously.

"I don't have to anymore," he said, and laughed.

He placed a rough hand on the back of her neck in a gesture that was both intimate and careless. She imagined each pore of her skin opening to receive his touch.

"I have to pick up Joey at his friend's house," he said gruffly. "I can't see you tonight."

"Tomorrow then," she answered lightly. "I'll be rooting for you."

"Tomorrow."

CHAPTER FOURTEEN

Mort Cunningham was a genial, easygoing man. It had been decided that he would do the running commentary and Nickie would do the color, sidelights, interviews, and statistical tidbits. The odds were stacked against Seattle in this, the last game of the season, but the pregame atmosphere remained festive. The team had played quite respectably this year.

Cunningham's commentary, as the game began, was flawless. Drawing on her phenomenal memory for anecdotes and a computer outlet for statistics, Nickie, too, played her part well, sometimes speaking directly on camera, sometimes passing Cunningham notes. She was careful not to try to steal the limelight, for her position today was as an adjunct.

When she went back to the dugout for player comments, the first thing to hit her eye was Joey sitting on the bench wearing a Viking cap that was much too large for him. He was munching on a hotdog. From the soggy look of the roll Nickie guessed that he had been holding it for a long time and that he was eating it to avoid offending the buyer rather than from hunger.

Craig came up to the boy, and put his hand on Joey's

shoulder. "Hello, Nicole. I guess you two have met before."

Nickie held her hand out to Joey. "I'm pleased to see you again, Joey. Craig has been telling me lots of nice things about you."

A curtain seemed to fall over his eyes as he looked at her. Nickie controlled an urge to put her arms around him. She knew only too well how lost and frightened Joey felt, and how the sight of any other woman of the same generation as his mother could remind him of his loss.

"You certainly were good, Joey. Everyone at the station loved you. Maybe you could come back sometime and do another interview for us."

"Excuse me, ma'am. Martins is up. I wanna see this."

Joey moved off to stand stiffly in front of the bench. Nickie stared after him helplessly.

"He needs some time. He's still licking his wounds," Craig said.

Nickie nodded. "I know."

"He'll do all right. He's a tough kid. And he'll have help—all the help he needs."

Nickie smiled at him, not the kind of smile where all you saw was a flash of white teeth, but a smile that came from her eyes and her heart. Intent on the action in the field, Craig missed it. Nickie, somewhat preoccupied, moved off to question several of the benched players. It was nice how easily they accepted her presence here—quite a contrast from her first encounter with them at the clubhouse. They gave her straight answers, seeming to choose their words, so that she was able to return to her seat in the press box armed with some nice quotes.

Craig pitched five innings. He was in top form and kept Cincinnati, even with their fine hitters, from scoring more than one run. Cincinnati more than made up for their poor start, however, when Seattle's relief pitcher came in. Nickie wondered how Craig was taking the change in score as Cincinnati got their fifth run in two innings! She knew it wasn't with equanimity. Deciding to ask him herself, she returned to the dugout. That would be just the kind of feedback viewers loved.

"Craig, over here!" she signaled to him.

"What can I do for you?"

"Answer a few questions."

He ambled over, his eyes still on the baseball diamond. "Shoot!"

"I love your arms," she whispered.

His attention was immediately riveted where she wanted it, on her.

"Er," she cleared her throat, "how do you feel about being out of the game? Do you wish they could put you back there on the mound?"

"Nah, the game's lost already. We wouldn't have made the national league playoffs even if we'd won. And I have to take care of the old arm."

He smiled roguishly, folding his arms over his chest while he looked down at the top of her shining hair. He seemed to be weighing something in his mind.

"Come with me. I want to show you something."

He led her in through the clubhouse to a small vestibule. One corner held a large hamper of dirty uniforms and clothing. A bar which stretched along one entire wall was hung with freshly cleaned uniforms, laundered jeans, and the many-hued bikini underwear that the players favored.

"Love the decor," Nickie commented dryly.

Craig took a key out of his pocket and inserted it in the lock of a door she had not even noticed, for its outlines blended well with the dusty green of the wall color. He beckoned her to follow him into a small, square room lined with posters of old-time players. There were two end tables holding bowls of sunflower seeds, chewing tobacco, and candy. There were leg weights, a hot tub, and a beat-up leather sofa.

"This is where we relax and where we play puck," Craig explained. Nickie knew that puck, a noisy variation of bridge, was a game peculiar to baseball players.

"Right now you're standing directly under the dugout," he continued.

"Do you mean to tell me that the team is sitting over my head?"

"Ever the inquiring reporter. Now about that interview . . ." He sank into the cracked leather sofa and patted a place next to him. Nickie's mouth curved into a mischievous smile. Still standing, she bent over him, her breath hot as she nibbled on his ear.

"Do you like this, Mr. Boone, or do you prefer your women demure?"

She nuzzled his neck and smoothed cool hands over his hard thighs. Craig looked at her with unbelieving eyes.

"I've heard of people who make love in Marie Antoinette's bedroom at Versailles but never in the trainer's room during the last game of the season!"

His voice betrayed a mix of laughter and excitement. With one quick movement he brought her down on his lap, wrapped his arms around her in a crushing embrace, and met her lips in a kiss that gave as much as it demanded. Nickie felt a jolt of shock course through her. Not sure of her intentions at the beginning, she felt now had before, mesmerized by his touch, completely His hands followed the lines and curves of his breath became audible. With precise hands he unbuttoned Nickie's shirt and pulled his own over his head. As she sat on his lap her eyes were level with his until with slow deliberateness he buried his face between her breasts. She covered his head with kisses, reveling in the silky feel of his black locks, so similar to her own. As he kissed her breasts and teased her nipples with his tongue all thoughts of the impropriety of the situation flew from her mind, and she found herself gripping his hair with her hands and uttering urgent female sounds. He lowered them both down to the sofa, she still on top. She kissed his chest, loving its heavily matted feel on her cheek.

"My beautiful, hungry darling. You're mine. I'll never let you go again."

Nickie covered his face with fluttery kisses. She helped as he tugged at her skirt. As he had done before, he stopped all movement to look at her, drinking in her naked charms. She felt that he was making love to her with his eyes. She knew that she pleased him, and that made her happier than she ever would have guessed. He divested himself of his pants and with deft expertise placed her on the sofa under him. She gave herself to him totally with every ounce of her strength and will and passion. She whimpered in ecstasy as their universe exploded in a kaleidoscope of color, sweetness, warmth, and wetness. When it was over he looked at her face in a long, searching gaze. She knew that he loved her.

"You drain me, my love. It's a good thing I don't pitch again until next season!"

"You give me too much credit."

"Maybe," he said with a grin, "I should make plans for an early retirement. We can spend the rest of our lives in bed!"

"We'd better get a Sealy Posturepedic!" Nickie laughed up at him.

"But meanwhile I haven't given you that interview yet. People might start wondering what went on in here if you go on the air empty-handed tonight. What would you say to a live interview?"

"You mean you'll come to the studio? Oh, Craig, that would be terrific. But you've always shunned that sort of thing like the plague. Are you sure you want to do it?"

"Only for you." As he spoke, Craig was throwing on his clothes. "You'd better get dressed. If somebody comes in, I don't know if they'd believe we were playing strip poker."

"I thought you locked the door," Nickie exclaimed.

"So I did. But it doesn't make much difference when everyone on the team has a key!"

"You're kidding!" Nickie jumped up and dressed in what couldn't have taken more than five seconds. "I ought to kill you for this," she scolded only half in jest.

Craig unlocked the door and held it open for her. "And this is the trainer's room," he said loudly. "Is there anything else I can do for you, Miss Alexander?"

"You've done more than enough, thank you," she retorted in an equally loud voice. "And you've been most helpful and instructive."

The players in the dugout barely noticed them as they emerged through the clubhouse door, though Nickie was sure that despite her best efforts she wore a sated, smug look. She turned to Craig.

"You'll be at the studio at five o'clock, then?"

"Right. And show me a little mercy with your questions!" She pursed her lips as if she were considering the request and saluted her agreement.

179

Deciding to wrap up this game with some words from the manager, Nickie tapped him on the shoulder to ask for a few minutes of his time. The short, stocky man took one look at Nickie and his glower turned from surly to threatening.

"Ain't got no time for the press."

"I beg your pardon?" Nickie raised her eyebrows incredulously. She noticed Craig listening with obvious interest. She used her most winning smile and professional manner to cajole the man to grant her the interview.

"Our fans out there will be very disappointed. *Sportswatch* brings the most exciting sports figures from the state of Washington into people's homes, as you know, and you of course are prominent among our heroes."

"Well, all right," the manager agreed grudgingly, "since you put it like that."

Nickie stole a glance at Craig, who was grinning from ear to ear. She suspected that he was thinking she had better not try any of that phony flattery on him! While the manager was momentarily occupied with reshuffling his schedule to fit her in, Nickie laughingly told Craig he was a pushover even without flattery.

"Only when I want to be," he returned.

Luckily, when the manager led her to a corner of the bench, she knew exactly which questions to ask to induce him to volubility. She asked him why he thought his record this year was so much better than last year's, what he was going to do next year to improve fielding, and if he anticipated any trades in the off season. Her only problem was in graciously ending the interview with the formerly taciturn manager.

She followed that interview up with a short, highly successful talk with the owner. With the live interview with Craig, she would have a super segment with which to end the baseball season!

Notes in hand, she returned to the press box, where Mort Cunningham was winding up his running commentary. She could barely keep her attention focused on the final plays for wanting to turn around and look at Craig in the dugout. The game ended with a seven-to-two loss for the Vikings. Though they hadn't made it to the playoffs or pennant, it had been a good season. The Vikings were improving rapidly. In the hustle of gathering equipment, last-minute notes, and finalizing arrangements for the broadcast with Mort (some of his commentary was to be reaired later), Nickie didn't have a chance to say anything more to Craig. She would see him next time, on camera.

CHAPTER FIFTEEN

"Miss Alexander." The doorman doffed his hat in greeting as Nickie strode purposefully into the studio.

"Hi, Nickie. How ya doin?" a sound technician boomed as she passed.

"Miss Alexander, will you sign this release, please." A young secretary ran up to her waving a paper and pen.

"There's a call waiting for you on four," another secretary said as she accosted Nickie and handed her a sheaf of papers marked urgent.

"I thought I told you to notify me as soon as Miss Alexander arrived," her elegant hairdresser lisped petulantly at the receptionist. He looked pointedly at his watch and frowned at Nickie, who hurried to the phone.

"What's that, a U.P. release?" Nickie asked sharply into the phone. "When? Right. Get me the details in time for the show."

The hairdresser stood with arms folded, looking pointedly at the wall clock. "If you please, unless you intend to look like you've been ransacking Filene's basement"—he named the famous Boston store—"you'll come with me."

Nickie followed him meekly. Recently imported from Massachusetts, Jean-Claude was the best hair stylist in the northwest, and if he thought her hair was a mess, then a mess it was. With the way Craig loved to run his fingers through her hair, it was a wonder she had managed to get it in any semblance of order.

Once in his chair, Nickie closed her eyes and let Jean-Claude work the wonders for which he had been hired. He coiled her hair in a sleek knot on top of her head, quite a feat considering her single-minded curls. A cosmetologist joined him to apply a mudpack to her face which left it tingling and fresh feeling. She followed up with a light application of base, powder, and eye makeup. Having heard all her life how lucky she was to have such big eyes and thick, lustrous lashes, Nickie had never bothered much with eye makeup. The results, the first time she had seen them, were dramatic and had taught her something about looks that she had always known about work: that very good could be better and very pretty could be prettier.

Rushing off to her dressing room, she waved off the secretaries who followed. This job was nothing if not hectic. She slipped into the peach linen suit that had been pressed by the studio valet, and checked herself in the mirror before leaving for the glass-enclosed interview set. It was furnished with potted palms, Breuer chairs, and a slate-top coffee table. Craig was already there munching on the bagel, cream cheese, and lox which was supplied gratis by the studio for all its guests before the show.

"Haven't I seen you somewhere recently? The outfit was different, I think." He grinned disarmingly.

"Perhaps you noticed me at the ball park. I was watching your every move."

"Are the mikes turned off?" he asked in a whisper.

Nickie nodded. "We have ten minutes before air time. Do you want to practice?"

Craig laughed. "I'm an expert already."

Fixing him with a ferocious stare, Nickie proceeded with a mock interview.

"Mr. Boone, your fans want to know, to what exactly do you attribute that flush on your face?"

"That's the flush of victory."

"Didn't your team lose?"

"They did, but I won a bigger prize."

"Though the Vikings lost, it was, wouldn't you agree, a very exciting game, Mr. Boone?"

"Indeed. Fireworks exploded."

"You have a reputation for a variety of pitches. Which is your favorite?"

"I like to take my time—smooth and easy." He winked. "Gets them every time."

"And your preferred position?"

"I'm a man who likes to be on top of things."

Nickie could no longer keep a straight face. "You'd better not say those things on the air!" she warned laughingly.

"Can I say I love you and want you to be my wife on the air?" Nickie turned to him, her pencil poised in midair. "Are you serious?"

"Do I sound like a comedian? I love you, Nicole. Do you love me?"

"Oh, I do."

"Sixty seconds to air time, Miss Alexander," a technician called.

"But what about my job?" she wailed. "It won't work out! I can't stay home all day, not now! And what about Joey?"

"I never said you had to stay home. And as for those glamorous jobs you've got your mind set on, we're not living in the eighteenth century. Didn't you ever hear of airplanes or telephones? If we have to live apart for a few days a week for a while we can work that out. It's been done. You just have to get over your fear of flying. And your fear of loving. As for Joey, he'll learn to love you, too, and the new brothers and sisters he'll have. That is, if you think you can grow to love him."

Her face wreathed in smiles, Nickie turned to camera number one, but not before she planted a kiss on Craig's lips and whispered a very soft "Yes, on all counts." She just had time, before the red light signaling that they were on the air flashed, to add an impish "The package does come complete with Jo-Jo, I hope?"

Craig grinned in amused exasperation.

"Good evening. Today ends Seattle's best season in twenty years. The scores in the final game were . . ."

LOOK FOR NEXT MONTH'S
CANDLELIGHT ECSTASY ROMANCES™

A love forged by destiny—
A passion born of flame

FLAMES OF DESIRE

by Vanessa Royall

Selena MacPherson, a proud princess of ancient
Scotland, had never met a man who did not desire
her. From the moment she met Royce Campbell at
an Edinburgh ball, Selena knew the burning
ecstasy that was to seal her fate through all eternity.
She sought him on the high seas, in India, and
finally in a young America raging in the
birth-throes of freedom, where destiny was bound
to fulfill its promise. . . .

A DELL BOOK $2.95

Come Faith, Come Fire

Vanessa Royall

Proud as her aristocratic upbringing, bold as the ancient gypsy blood that ran in her veins, the beautiful golden-haired Maria saw her family burned at the stake and watched her young love, forced into the priesthood. Desperate and bound by a forbidden love, Maria defies the Grand Inquisitor himself and flees across Spain to a burning love that was destined to be free!

A Dell Book $2.95 **(12173-6)**

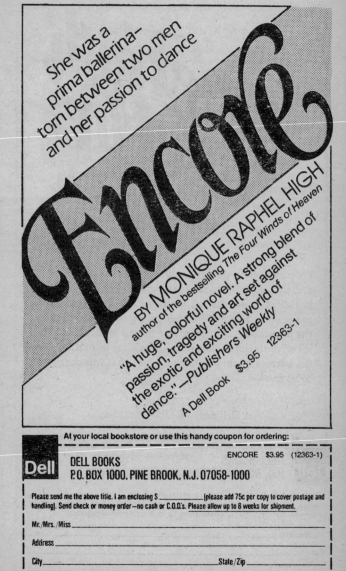

She was a
prima ballerina—
torn between two men
and her passion to dance

Encore

BY MONIQUE RAPHEL HIGH
author of the bestselling *The Four Winds of Heaven*

"A huge, colorful novel. A strong blend of
passion, tragedy and art set against
the exotic and exciting world of
dance." —*Publishers Weekly*

A Dell Book $3.95   12363-1